CHARADE

BS GILL

LITTLE TORCH

Little Torch Publishing

ISBN 978-1-8381215-0-1

We can never cease to be ourselves.

Joseph Conrad, The Secret Agent

1

Lewis Pritchard looked like any other middle-aged man driving to work on a Monday morning. The traffic out of London was light, and his car was one of many, headlights streaming through the rain, that sped along the motorway. He turned off the radio and fell deep into thought. This would be the last chance he would have to relax and clear his mind before another busy day.

His finely tailored grey suit, clean pressed white shirt, and determined expression would not have been out of place in a large accountancy firm where he may have been a senior partner. But he was not a staid accountant interested in balancing columns of numbers in a spreadsheet or finding tax loopholes for wealthy clients; he was a man whose decisions were much more significant. Indeed, on many occasions, decisions made by him had meant the difference between life and death.

He turned the steering wheel, peeled off the motorway and was soon navigating the narrow residential streets of Cheltenham. Finally, he reached the perimeter road, which encircled the office complex where he worked, slowed his car to a halt as he reached the checkpoint and dimmed the headlights. He drew down the window as a uniformed guard, his face white and cold, stepped up to the barrier, and as Pritchard had done every working day for the past ten years, held out his ID for inspection. The guard rapidly glanced at the card and then back at Pritchard before signalling to a colleague sitting in a small hut. The pole swung up, and the guard waved the car through.

Pritchard pulled up in his designated parking bay and sat for a moment listening to the patter of rain on the windscreen before snapping off the engine, grabbing his briefcase from the passenger's seat and getting out. The rain which had been falling in sheets when he had left home half an hour ago was now no more than a drizzle.

Drops of rain dribbled down his hard, lean face—a face that never yielded to even a ghost of a smile—as he took a moment to look up at the vast office complex which towered above him, his cold breath mushrooming in his face. The four-storey structure blocked out the grey clouds, smeared like grease across the bleak horizon. The windows of the outer corridors were all illuminated, their reflections caught in puddles on the tarmac. The night shift was coming to an end; reports and status updates were being handed over to the day staff.

It was ironic, he thought, how an organisation that prized secrecy above all else occupied a building with so many windows. He preferred the security of cold brick walls between him and the outside world.

His piercing, blue eyes lit up his face. It was an unsettling, intense look, almost fanatical. He took a moment every morning to pause and look up at the office, even when it rained, wanting to savour the fact that he, a poor boy from an East London council estate, had made it to the top echelons of GCHQ. It had been a long and distinguished career, he thought. He checked himself. It was far from being over. At only forty-five, there was a lot he still would achieve. Faint pride stirred within him at the thought that one day his portrait would adorn the staircase in some prestigious government building in Whitehall. Of that, he had no doubt.

His briefcase was taken from him at the security desk by a stony-faced guard who put it on the conveyor belt to be scanned by an X-ray machine. Plastered on the walls were signs prohibiting unauthorised electronic equipment and reminding staff of their duty to report anything suspicious. There was no special privilege given to rank or status at the security desk; he was just another employee, another possible security risk.

But once Pritchard was past security, he was not just another employee but a man of importance responsible for the running of K Division: the Chinese signals intelligence station.

He walked along the circular walkway, which ran through the centre of the atrium. High above, rain pattered against the slanted glass roof. On reaching the lift, he pressed the button and waited for it to descend. Several junior members of staff walked past, nodding and bidding him good morning, but he made no reciprocal gesture. For him, respect was a one-way street; he had earned it, these nameless minions had not.

As the lift ascended, he looked down through the glass door at the clean white high-gloss-marble reception desk, surrounded by a sea of brilliant white stone flooring, overlooked by balconies with steel handrails that glinted under spotlights. At the centre of the building—or Doughnut as it was commonly known, owing to its geometric resemblance to the dessert—was a circular open-air garden courtyard, intended as a place of contemplation and relaxation. The ground was sodden; it would not be used today. He didn't care for it; it was full of nasty insects, which aggravated his allergies. He would have preferred to live in a concrete world devoid of nature.

Ensconced behind his office desk, he took a sip from a mug of hot chocolate, his one concession to comfort, and took the topmost dossier, left by the night staff, from the pile on his desk. Unclipping its cover, he opened it, took out the sheets one at a time, giving each a cursory glance before returning to the first one and began reading it in earnest.

What he read were intercepted email and telephone transcripts detailing the detention of a dissident journalist in Wuhan. There would be no trial or hearing into his alleged offences and no newspaper report or mention on the Chinese side of the internet. It would not be long before friends and relatives of the man would realise what had happened and break the news on the free internet. Only then would it be picked up by the western newspapers. But this would be of little help to the dissident. He would disappear, taken away for re-education in some remote part of the country, and it would be years before he was heard of again, if ever.

It was a routine matter and something that happened almost every day. In a population of over a billion, did one fewer person make a difference? Pritchard couldn't fathom what possessed people to make martyrs of themselves. He was grateful that he had been spared any ideological indoctrination as a child. His formative years focused on getting ahead and dealing with practical problems such as finding a place to live and earning enough money to pay rent.

The world, he thought, would be a better place without these ideological dreamers.

His musings were cut short by an electronic beep from his computer. He tapped on the keyboard and read the message that flashed up on his screen, scowling as he did so. It was a reminder that his attendance tonight at Jason Black's leaving party was expected. He was annoyed that what he considered a frivolous message should be sent through their secure system.

He would have to call his wife, who had probably forgotten about it. God, how he hoped she had not already hit the bottle. He looked at the framed photograph of her on his desk. It was his only personal possession in the office but one which was conspicuously placed. The shelves were crammed full of thick directories, and the walls were covered in schematics and maps. But there could be no missing the photograph. He didn't want there to be any doubt in anyone's mind that he was married, and from the smiling faces of himself and his wife, happily so.

He turned his attention back to the file. But he hadn't read another word before there was another beep. Again, he tapped on his keyboard to bring up the message. This time he stared at the screen, his mouth slack with amazement.

2

Lyle Anderson, head of MI5's A Branch, did his best to appear interested in what the Home Secretary said, nodding his head and interjecting the occasional 'Of course, that's only to be expected' and 'I'll get back to you on that point'.

It had been a relaxed meeting; the Home Secretary surprisingly sympathetic. This was not what Anderson had expected. He had anticipated that she would rake him over the coals. A Branch was responsible for covert entry, audio and video surveillance, and intercept transcription. And as such, there was an overlap with the activities with its sister organisation, GCHQ. Ever since Edward Snowden had leaked thousands of classified documents for the world's edification, it had been a process of damage limitation for both agencies. Anderson had assured the Home Secretary that they were over the worst of it. Hence, she was sanguine about the whole matter. Besides, she was clear in her mind about who was the real villain of the piece.

Anderson stifled a yawn, feeling tired and every one of his sixty years. The Whitehall office was hot, too hot. The plush leather armchair in which he sat was too comfortable, and he was finding it difficult to keep his eyes open. Taking another sip of his tea which was too sweet, he found his mind wandering ahead to Jason Black's leaving bash. A furtive glance at his watch revealed that it was eleven o'clock. It was going to be a long day.

So, he was glad for the interruption when his phone beeped. As he read the encrypted email, not the faintest trace of emotion registered on his broad, tanned face. Putting the phone back in his pocket, he apologised for the interruption and leant back in his chair, allowing the Home Secretary to drone on. However, now he had no problem keeping awake—his mind racing as it processed the message's contents.

He wasted no time in pleasantries when all the business of the meeting had been concluded, immediately excusing himself. Five minutes later, his chauffeur-driven car was racing up to Cheltenham. Sitting bolt upright in the back, he took out his phone and shook his head as he reread the message.

Anderson stormed past a huddle of workers loitering around a water cooler. He threaded his way between the ranks of linguists and administrative staff at their desks, hunched over keyboards, poring over paperwork. Pritchard, his body tense, stood by his desk, watching Anderson through the glass panel in the door. The door swung open.

Slightly breathless, Anderson said, "Any more details?"

Without saying a word, Pritchard handed him a sheet of paper.

Anderson read the transcript, deep furrows in his brow becoming more pronounced with each word he read. Here, with his own people, he didn't hold back his emotions.

Slamming the sheet down on Pritchard's desk, he said, "Bruce Taylor. That's a name I never thought I'd ever hear again."

Pritchard remained silent, brooding.

Anderson said, "And Clean Start! That was your bird, wasn't it?"

"It was as much yours as ours," Pritchard snapped back.

Pritchard walked over to the window, his mind in tumult.

Anderson said, "He's been missing for three years, and he turns up in a psychiatric hospital. You couldn't make it up. It's as if it's been taken straight out of the pages of a spy novel."

Pritchard spun around and said, "The whole thing's got a bad smell to it. Whoever this person really is, we need to contain the situation."

"You don't think it is Taylor?"

"I don't know."

"Who then?"

Pritchard stared at Anderson and said, "How can a person disappear for three years? It's not possible to go completely off the grid for that length of time. And why would he? It's not as if he had any reason to go into hiding. No, someone knows about Clean Start. I think we're being played. And we're screwed if this ever gets out."

Anderson considered and said, "Talking of the proverbial shaft. I've just come from a meeting with the Home Secretary."

"Oh, I suppose Snowden was still on the agenda."

"Yes, the very top. I assured her that we were over the worst of it and that there wouldn't be any new revelations."

"You think Snowden might have stolen intelligence on Clean Start?"

"I don't know. There were thousands of documents he copied onto his memory stick. *The Guardian's* probably still trawling through them."

"You don't seem too worried about it."

"I'm not. If they had even a sniff of what Clean Start was, they would have already run with it. They don't have an iota of patriotism. An assassination programme is a lot sexier than phone taps, and it sells a lot more copy. That's all they care about."

"If they have got something—fuck! The Home Secretary's patience isn't infinite. She's onside at the moment, but that can change in the blink of an eye. She won't stand at the dispatch box and defend murder. She'd throw us all under the bus in a heartbeat."

"Then let's hope we can keep a lid on this."

"It's not going to be easy. These things spread like a contagion. Right now, there's a shrink, Dr Peters, prodding and poking about in Taylor's mind—or whoever it is."

"I'll send someone to the hospital."

"There's no need; I already have."

"You sent one of *your* officers?"

"Yes. Anne Richmond."

"Are you sure she's up to it? No offence, but your lot are really just translators and code breakers. I can talk with Johnson and get someone from G Branch. They've got experience. They—"

"We're a mature department; we can manage. Her file flagged her up as a reliable officer who'll get the job done without complications. In fact, she used to work for D Branch and has experience of fieldwork."

"Yes?"

"She transferred a year ago."

A faint recollection stirred in Anderson's mind. He had heard her name before, but he couldn't pin down where.

He said, "What is she?"

"A linguist—Russian speaker."

"How much did you tell her?"

"I didn't tell her anything. Barnes briefed her. He told her what she needed to know and no more."

"You haven't spoken to her?"

"No."

"How can you be sure she's up to it? You can't get everything from a file."

"There wasn't time!"

Or desire or inclination, Anderson thought. He could not understand Pritchard's aversion to human contact and wondered, what made a man this cold?

Looking down at the framed photograph on the desk, he found it hard to believe that Pritchard had such a beautiful wife. What was the attraction? What did she see in him? Surely, it was not just money and prestige? But the world was a harsh place, and she would not have been the first woman to have sacrificed herself for financial security.

Pritchard said, "Her part's straightforward. She's posing as his sister and just has to ID him, evaluate the premises to see if they're secure and then report back."

Anderson took a moment to consider.

He said, "Maybe we shouldn't wait; just send a team in now to get Taylor out of there."

"Let's not rush things. We don't want to rouse any suspicions. The Russians may have set this whole thing up. We don't want to walk into a trap."

"But—"

"Trust me on this. It's the best way to proceed."

"If you think she can handle it—"

"She can."

Anderson glanced through the office's glass partition at the staff working outside and said, "You know, the whole point of this building—when they decided on making it open-plan—was to encourage cooperation and have more face-to-face meetings."

Pritchard frowned. He didn't appreciate that his office was only separated from the rest of the floor by a thin glass partition, and he longed to be back in the bland concrete offices in Oakley with its narrow corridors. A person could spend years there working alone in his office and never know—or care—what the person next door was doing. Everyone was left to get on with their work. But 'modern' thinking deemed it necessary to have a more open architecture because, as it was said, everyone had something to contribute.

"I'll do things my way," he said.

Anderson shrugged and said, "How is she going to explain how she knew he was in the hospital?"

"She already has. She phoned ahead. There was an incident in the town centre when Taylor was picked up. He was walking around, dazed and confused and got into a fight. She has a cover story about a friend, working for a local rag, who gave her the hospital's name. Hopefully, they'll buy it."

"They're just doctors. Why would they get suspicious? To them, he's just another headcase."

"Let's hope they are *just* doctors."

"Your suspicion knows no bounds?"

"Nor should it. We've both been in this business too long."

"I think you're seeing trouble where there isn't any."

"Maybe, but I'll feel better after she reports back."

"And if he *really* is Taylor?"

Pritchard said nothing.

Anderson added, "You know, we put a lot of resources into Clean Start and never got the results we wanted. Speculation is that somebody tipped off the Russians that Taylor was on his way to Stonebridge, and that's how they got to him."

Pritchard said, "That's the easiest excuse to make. Somebody up on high screwed up, and they're covering for him. The old school tie and all that."

All his life, Pritchard had carried bitterness in his heart. He first felt the anger and bile rise in him when, even after achieving outstanding grades in his A-levels, he had been unsuccessful in gaining entry into any of the Oxbridge colleges and had to settle for one of the redbrick universities. This injustice was something for which he would never forgive society as a whole. And because of this failure, he had had to work even harder to get to the top. There had been no favours he could call in or old school tie to assist him in his ascent. In his eyes, he had succeeded in spite of everyone.

"Charters took it badly," Anderson said.

"He was to blame!" Pritchard said. "He had a reputation for being reckless when he was an officer, and that hasn't changed now that he's got the top job. His ideas are too risky. Over seven officers have gone missing on his watch this past year."

"I know."

"You remember the one who was found floating in the Volga last year? That was one of his bright ideas, another joint black op we had to close down. He's a loose cannon. He only got the job because he went to Eton with the PM."

"Even so, he's not going to want a stink on this one. Everything's got to go by the numbers."

3

Dr Peters let out a high-pitched whistle from between his teeth and said, "This is for real?"

Dr Campbell, a fresh-faced graduate in his first appointment since leaving university, smiled and answered, "It's no wind-up. I got the email this morning. He'll be coming in on the twelve-thirty train. I'll send a porter to meet him at the station."

Peters leant back in his chair and brushed back his soft brown hair from his boyish face that had seemingly not grown a day older from when he had graduated from medical school six years earlier.

"Professor Belakovsky," he said. "I can't believe it. It's all so out of the blue. I had no idea he was even in the country. I thought he was working in Switzerland."

"He's been doing research at Sussex University. Jeff must have forwarded him your email about Taylor."

"Well, I'll have to buy Jeff a beer the next time I see him. Hell, I'll buy him lunch at the Savoy. I thought if I could get Jeff here, that would be great. But Belakovsky—this is the biggest thing that's ever happened here."

There had been a nagging worry in Peters' mind, ever since he had accepted the job at Mountview Hospital, that he might have made a mistake. It had seemed like a sensible career move at the time to become the head of a department, but he now realised that there was a great deal of snobbery within the medical community, and few academics took anything from a doctor working in a small rural hospital seriously. What papers he had published on the internet and in journals had been largely ignored. But that would all change now with the news of Belakovsky's arrival.

Campbell said, "You'd be happy to hand Taylor's case over to him?"

Peters threw up his arms.

"God, yeah. He can work with any patient he likes. There's so much I can learn from him. There's a rumour that he'll finally get the Nobel Prize for his work on prion damage. It won't do any of our careers any harm if we say we worked with the great Belakovsky. It's the kind of thing that opens doors. When he does—"

The phone on Peters' desk rang, and he picked up the receiver.

"Peters. Yes. OK. I'll be down in a minute."

He hung up.

"Taylor's sister is here."

Anne Richmond drove through the undulating Yorkshire countryside, the chill wind rushing in through the half-open window. As of yet, the heavy rain which had been forecast had not materialised, although ominous dark clouds were gathering in the distance.

As she drove over the brow of a hill, she saw the spire of the hospital chapel. The hospital was isolated, surrounded by fields and was a five-minute drive to the nearest town. Cows grazed in the fields, and starlings perched on trees watched in hunched silence as her car sped past.

The hospital was hidden behind a forbiddingly high brick wall, but Anne caught a glimpse of the two-storey, red-brick Victorian building through the entrance archway. It was an elegant building with a quaint, old-world quality about it.

However, it had been somewhat spoilt by anachronistic alarms, security doors and barred windows.

She drove under the archway and followed the signs to the car park at the side of the hospital. It was empty, except for two cars parked in the designated staff area. As Anne got out of her car, she took out a small photograph and studied it for a moment before slipping it back into her pocket.

The reception was of a generic design with a thin, low pile carpet, beige walls and pine furniture. A prudish-looking secretary sat behind a semi-circular desk, staring at a computer monitor, her salt and pepper hair tied in an efficient bun. She stopped typing and peered over the rim of her half-moon reading glasses balanced on the tip of her nose when Anne entered.

"Can I help you?"

"I'm here to see Dr Peters."

"Your name?"

"Claire Taylor."

The receptionist picked up the phone on her desk.

It was a short wait for Anne before Peters loped into the room. The two of them cordially shook hands and then made their way down the corridor that led to the ward.

Peters said, "I'm still not clear about how you knew your brother was here?"

"I have a friend who works at the *Gazette.*"

"How did he know?"

"He has sources who check up on these things."

Peters smiled, a glint in his eyes.

He said, "It all sounds very mysterious. These journalists have their ways. They call them the black arts, don't they?"

"I wouldn't know. I don't really know much about it."

Peters stopped at a metal security door and quickly tapped in the entry code on the keypad. The door opened.

"Are the patients here dangerous?"

"Not in this wing. The patients on this side are voluntary admissions. They want help. The only reason for the locked door is to stop them from wandering off. We have to give some of them quite powerful drugs, and it can confuse them. But you can put your mind at ease about your brother; he's getting the best possible treatment."

"What exactly's wrong with him?"

"Amnesia coupled with a delusion. We need to investigate the cause. I've taken scans to see if there's been any trauma."

"Has there?"

"Not that I can see. But it's not just a simple matter of looking at an X-ray or MRI scan. Sometimes physical damage can heal, superficially, but there's lasting damage beneath the surface."

"What if there's no trauma?"

"There may be a psychological cause. But that's something we can talk about after you've seen him. I want you to be assured we're doing all we can."

They came to another security door. Again, Peters opened it with a few taps on a keypad.

"What kind of delusion is he having?"

"He talks about being a secret agent."

"Oh?"

Peters smiled and said, "It's not that uncommon."

"You've dealt with this kind of thing before?"

"Not specifically spies and agents, but I did have a patient a few years ago who thought he was a general."

"And he wasn't?"

Peters laughed.

"No. He was a plumber. His wife had been driving him to work. He was playing a video game—some army strategy game—when their car crashed. The last thing he remembered was being in command of the Normandy invasions. He kept going on for days about how he was needed at Command HQ. He snapped out of it, and there was no permanent damage.

"It's a kind of defence mechanism the mind has. If there's a gaping hole in a person's memories, there's a need to fill it with something—often fantasies and desires the person may have had."

They reached the end of the corridor and entered the ward. Its freshly mopped linoleum floor was still damp in patches. Two male patients were sitting in high-back chairs, rapt, their attention on the TV, showing a daytime chat show.

Peters' face darkened, and he said, "He must be in his room. I was hoping he would spend more time in the day area."

They walked over to a door.

Peters turned to Anne and said, "You have to understand that his amnesia is total. He probably won't remember you at all."

"You didn't tell him I was coming?"

"I told him he had a visitor but not that you're his sister. I want him to try and remember things naturally. It's important that he isn't simply told everything. Don't be upset if he doesn't remember you."

"I won't be."

"I thought, afterwards, we could go to my office and run over a few details and discuss how to move forward with his treatment. I'd like you to play as full a part as possible, and I'm sure you have a lot of questions you want to ask."

Peters knocked on the door.

4

Bruce Taylor sat in a high-backed chair staring out of the window, watching a nurse wearing a plain white uniform push a patient in a wheelchair along a winding path that ran down to the hospital's perimeter wall. The nurse stopped at a flowerbed, giving the patient, an emaciated young man wrapped in a duffle coat, an opportunity to take a closer look at an azalea shrub. The patient's trembling fingers reached out to touch the blood-red flowers. The nurse looked up at the darkening sky; the wind was starting to pick up.

The patient has an illness that's clear for all to see, Taylor thought. His body, weak and frail, won't last much longer. He'll soon have his release from pain. I won't. When I leave this place—as I will have to—people will see a man no different from any other. They will not see my pain—hidden as it is in my mind. Yet, every day, I'll be as afraid as I am now.

He was glad for the brick wall that blocked out the nearby town's houses, which ran up the distant hills. The less he could see of the world, the safer he felt. A part of him wanted to draw the curtains and put another barrier between him and the outside. For him, the world was a frightening place where everyone was a stranger. Without his memories, he was even a stranger to himself. But he also knew that to live like a prisoner in this room was not to live at all.

He remembered shreds and fragments from his childhood, but there was a gaping black hole of decades to his next memory. That had been two weeks ago when his eyelids had flickered open, the biting cold autumnal wind cutting across his face. It had been early evening and already dark. He was sitting on a park bench, dried leaves blowing about his feet. Around him, shoppers weighed down by bags filled to bursting were briskly walking past, the occasional one glancing at him.

He ran his hand through his thick, bushy beard and slowly began to take in his surroundings, his body awakening from what felt like a long sleep. He was in a small park set slightly apart from a busy thoroughfare. Stretching his arms, he yawned and then looked down at his clothes: jeans, T-shirt and a jacket, worn and threadbare, with blotches of old food stains. He Pulled up the lapel of his jacket, sniffed it, grimaced and let go; it reeked of alcohol.

Hauling himself to his feet, he unsteadily made his way out of the park, not knowing where he was going, just needing to move, to do something.

The bright shopfront displays and lights dazzled him. Buffeted by a sea of shoppers, he walked on, his body stiff and aching. The tired faces of office workers flashed past him as they pressed and jostled against one another, making their way down the narrow subway stairs.

Everything around him was loud and discordant, and he felt short of breath and closed in by the people around him. Catching sight of the reflection of a dishevelled tramp in a shop window, he stepped closer, scrutinising it, running his hand over his face, only half believing it was him.

Now, the question finally came to him like a bolt from the blue. Who am I? He had no idea, no memory at all. How had he got here? Again, he had no idea. Fear seized him, and he frantically rummaged through his pockets but found only a half-crumpled packet of cigarettes and a bus ticket. He glanced around, the tumult of the traffic rising up in his mind.

Who am I? Who am I? He clasped his ears and wanted to scream. He broke into a run; he had to get away and find somewhere quiet where he could think and try to remember. However, he ran straight into the back of a man drinking a can of cola. The two of them tumbled to the pavement. Taylor sat up. Dazed, he looked up to find himself staring into a red, scowling face, cola dribbling down its jowls.

The man threw a punch, but Taylor managed to roll to one side and avoid being hit. Both men scrambled to their feet. The man swore and threw himself on Taylor.

Even now, sitting in his room a week later, Taylor could not remember what happened next. All he remembered was standing over the man lying unconscious in the gutter, blood trickling from his ear.

A group of curious shoppers formed a huddle around the two men. Taylor looked at their faces; some frightened, their mouths agape, others with eyes wide with excitement.

"I didn't mean to hurt him," Taylor said to no one in particular.

He sat down on the pavement next to the prostrate man and patiently waited for the police, the onlookers keeping a wary distance from him. Feeling faint, he closed his eyes. The next time he opened them, he was sitting in this very room in the hospital.

Peters had reassured him that the man had made a full recovery and that his injuries were not as bad as they appeared.

"You've seen him?" Taylor asked.

"No, the policemen who brought you here told me everything. What's important is that you rest and try to recover your strength. You've been through a lot. You need to get into a routine. Things will come back to you. Try not to overthink them."

With this stock phrase, he ended all their talks. It was as if he believed that thinking was something to which patients should be averse, something that should be left only to the professionals.

Peters spent half an hour during his rounds every morning talking with Taylor, but nothing was learnt or accomplished, and so, for most of the day, Taylor was left to brood in his room. He kept aloof from the other patients, most of whom were heavily medicated. Apart from the TV—which quickly bored him—there were few distractions to keep his mind occupied and stop it from returning to the central question of his identity, which dominated his thoughts.

On his fourth day in the hospital, Taylor awoke from an afternoon nap and remembered his name, along with the words Clean Start and Stonebridge. He rushed to tell Peters, who was excited by the breakthrough and felt vindicated in his slowly-slowly approach.

That evening, Peters made enquiries at nearby homeless shelters; Clean Start sounded to him like a rehabilitation programme run by a charity. However, enquiries proved a dead end. Even so, at least they now knew his name. Peters reassured Taylor that he would make more enquiries and get to the bottom of things, but he made no subsequent breakthroughs.

Since being admitted, Taylor had had several vivid nightmares, and one, in particular, kept recurring. In it, a man, sitting in a car, was pleading with him. The man spoke German—a language Taylor did not understand—and kept looking down at his chest, which was hidden by the car door.

This dream always left Taylor feeling uneasy and on edge when he awoke. Fear of revealing something horrible about his past, about himself, stopped him from telling Peters about any of his dreams, but he did tell Peters that he believed he was a secret agent. There was no concrete reason for this belief; it was just a feeling that he had. To his surprise, Peters had not dismissed the possibility.

He said, "I'll look into it. I think you're making real progress. In the meantime, try and let things come back naturally. Try not to force the issue."

Taylor broke from his deliberations when he heard a woman's voice outside. His body became tense. The realisation that his visitor was a woman completely threw him. What if he was married? For some reason, he had not considered the possibility until now. The idea that he could have a wife and even children seemed surreal.

There was a knock, and the door creaked open. Taylor heard the tap of heels on the linoleum floor.

"Bruce, your visitor's here," Peters said.

Taylor braced himself, got to his feet and turned around. He was pleasantly surprised by the woman. In fact, he found her to be very beautiful and felt there was safety in beauty. However, he had no memory of her.

He looked across at Peters, who was watching him with studied curiosity, and then back at Anne.

"I'll give you two some privacy," Peters said. "Please bear in mind what we talked about outside."

"I will," Anne said.

Peters left and closed the door.

Anne and Taylor stood for a moment, staring at each other. Taylor thought, how does one begin to piece together a life which, for all intents and purposes, will never be more than a hazy memory.

Anne went over to the door and listened intently. She glanced back at Taylor and smiled self-consciously.

"I want to make sure we're alone."

5

The middle-aged couple looked expectantly, hopefully at Peters, who had a lot of experience of reassuring anxious parents. His soothing bedside manner was well-rehearsed and effective, and he didn't overpromise the benefits of any treatment and hence come across as insincere.

The dour father wore a blue flannel suit. Sitting beside him, his stout wife, her hands folded on her lap, wearing a tweed jacket and skirt. They had been very formal and reserved throughout the meeting in Peters' office.

Peters leafed through the notes on his clipboard. The case was a standard one. Indeed, it could have been taken straight from the pages of a psychiatric textbook: a girl from a comfortable middle-class home suffering from an acute nervous breakdown. She was mature enough to be leading her own life but was stuck at home in an oppressive environment where her parents laid down rules which did nothing but add to her feelings of inadequacy.

He would treat the girl but doubted he would find a tactful way to broach his main concern that they, the parents, were the root cause of the problem. From past experience, he doubted they would accept this fact.

If he did put forward this hypothesis, there was the real possibility that the parents would become defensive, leave, and admit their daughter to another hospital. Hence a vicious cycle of cure and relapse would follow. Each episode of the girl's anxiety would result in a new hospital admission, apparent cure, and then relapse after being discharged and spending a few weeks back in the oppressive home environment. Over time, her condition would deteriorate.

Peters said, "We have very experienced staff working here. As it happens, Professor Belakovsky is arriving later today."

The name meant nothing to the couple. The father started to fidget with his tie while the mother fussed with her hands. Peters, slightly deflated by the lack of a response, returned his gaze to his clipboard.

The father cleared his throat and said, "What are the risks? We don't want her to suffer."

"Oh, you can put your mind at ease about that. I don't think we'll need to do anything drastic."

"Are you going to do that electric therapy?"

Peters smiled.

"Psychiatry has moved on a lot. ECT—that's what you're thinking about—is only ever used as a last resort. From the brief talk that I've had with your daughter, I think a lot of the time will be spent with talking therapies.

"Talking?"

"Yes, CBT. Cognitive Behavioural Therapy. We talk with the patient and try to identify the causes of their illness."

Peters paused before adding, "They're not always what we'd like to hear."

The father knitted his eyebrows.

"What do you mean?"

"Sometimes, the environment the patient lives in can be a cause of much stress."

The father's face coloured.

"You mean us?"

Peters felt tense; he loathed confrontation.

"I have to take into account all possibilities. I wouldn't be surprised if, in your daughter's case, it's something of her own making. For instance, a secret or feeling that she's suppressing."

"Emily has no secrets!" the mother exclaimed.

The father clasped his wife's hand.

"The doctor's only talking in general terms, dear."

Peters had feared an outburst. It was precisely this kind of fussing, he felt, that was the cause of their daughter's illness. If only he could make them see.

The father looked to Peters like a stuck-up half-colonel, detached from his emotions and a slave to protocol and duty. The wife and daughter's roles were set in stone to be dutiful helpers.

The mother looked pleadingly at Peters, and his aversion to confrontation prevailed.

"Yes," he said. "These are just generalisations. I'm sure Emily has no secrets. Let's see how the therapy goes."

The father said, "What about those patients outside? They seem a bit out of it."

"The effects of the medications can often look worse than they are."

"How long will it take?"

"A few weeks."

"We'll be able to visit?"

"Of course. I'll show you around the hospital. There's no reason to be worried."

The parents got up and followed Peters into the ward. The father took Peters to one side.

"Emily's our adopted daughter. All that talk of secrets just brought that back to my wife. She doesn't like to be reminded."

"Oh, I didn't realise. I'm sorry."

Peters looked across the ward at Taylor, his thoughts momentarily returning to his meeting with Anne shortly after her talk with Taylor. She had spoken about him as if he had been a stranger. She seemed to know nothing at all about him. Indeed, she even had to take a second when he asked her for his date of birth. They had evidently not been close. He hoped, for Taylor's sake, that they would be closer now. He would need at least one person he could turn to after leaving the hospital's relative safety. Illness, Peters reflected, had a way of bringing people together and putting past differences to one side. He hoped it would be true for them.

The sound of a cough broke him from his train of thought.

"The guided tour," he said, smiling.

He led the parents down the corridor.

6

"They're my parents."

Taylor, who had been watching Peters and the middle-aged couple, turned to the girl who had noiselessly taken up the seat beside him.

She was a petite creature, staring fixedly at him with intense dark brown almond-shaped eyes. Her face was a pleasant fusion of oriental and European features, framed by silky, black hair. She was dressed casually in a T-shirt and jeans.

Taylor, his mind sluggish and tired, was at a loss for a response.

The girl said, "They haven't juiced you up, have they?"

"No, I'm just a bit worn out."

The girl smiled.

"I'm Emily."

"Taylor."

"That's an unusual name."

"Bruce is my first name. Bruce Taylor."

Emily stared across the ward at Peters, who was leading her parents down the corridor.

She said, "I guess they're in for the guided tour with all the bells and whistles. Peters is very proud of this place. I don't suppose it's all smiles, though."

The smile disappeared from her face as she turned to look at the two docile patients propped up in front of the TV, drool dripping from their slack mouths onto their hospital gowns. Taylor followed her gaze.

She said, "I wonder if that's what he's got in store for me—for us."

"He said they have psychotic episodes and can get quite violent. They're getting better."

"Better just means more manageable, compliant. They wouldn't be doing any better if they were lobotomised. Look at them staring at the TV."

Taylor could not help but agree. It was a pitiful sight and somewhat upsetting.

"You don't trust him?" he said.

"He seems pleasant enough."

She smiled, her happy disposition returning as quickly as it had departed and said, "How long have you been here?"

"Two weeks."

"What's wrong with you?"

Taylor considered.

"I didn't mean to pry. If you don't want to talk about—"

"No, it's not that. I was trying to … I've got amnesia."

"Have you had it long?"

"As long as I can remember."

They both burst into laughter.

Strange, Taylor thought. He could not remember the last time he had laughed. He was sure it was not something he had done a lot in the past.

"So, you don't remember anything about who you are?"

Taylor shook his head.

"Not really. It was only a few days ago that I remembered my name. That and Clean Start."

"Clean Start?"

"It's a phrase that keeps coming up in my mind. I don't know what it means."

He ran his hand through his beard and said, "I'm not even sure this belongs."

"It makes you look old. I think you should shave it off."

"That's something I can talk about with Belakovsky."

"Who?"

"Professor Belakovsky. He's a world-famous psychiatrist. He's arriving today to take over my treatment."

"My parents think I'm neurotic."

"You seem OK to me."

"It comes and goes. When I meet someone new, it takes the edge off things."

"Don't worry about the treatment. It really is just a lot of talking."

"That's what Peters said. I feel better about it, now that I've got you to talk with."

She smiled again.

Taylor felt his heart miss a beat. It was painful for him to think of that cheerful, little face ever experiencing pain. Yet, she must be in pain to have been admitted here. How easy it is to hide one's feelings behind a smile, he thought.

Emily said, "There can't be many things worse than being locked up without having done anything wrong. When do you think they'll let you out?"

"They're not keeping me. I want to stay—as long as I can."

"You do? Why?"

"Before I came here, I was wandering about in the high street. I was afraid. I didn't even know how I'd got there. I didn't know anyone. People kept staring at me. Everyone was so strange and unfriendly. I looked like a tramp. I guess people don't see you as a human being when you're down and out. These aren't even my clothes. Peters bought them for me. I got into a fight. I was so scared. You're the first friendly person I've met since I've been here."

"But you said Peters—"

"Oh, he's friendly, but that's part of his job."

"So, you do think there's more to him?"

"I have to trust people. I'm not going to get better if I see enemies everywhere. I wish I could meet some of my old friends."

"Do you think you had many?"

"I don't know. I like to think so."

A shadow fell over his face, and he said, "Maybe I don't. What if I wasn't a nice person? For all I know, I could've been a monster."

A chill ran down his spine as the pleading man in his dream rose up before him.

"A monster," Taylor muttered, half lost in thought.

"No," Emily said, shaking her head. "I don't believe that. You've got a kind face."

"If only it were that simple."

"Would you still want to remember even if your past was bad?"

"Yes. If I've done bad things in my life, I'd like to make amends. The past doesn't exist just in my mind. It's real. If people have been affected by what I've done, this could be a second chance for me."

"So, you've got no idea what you used to do?"

"No. My sister came to visit me today. I didn't recognise her. It's funny."

"What is?"

"She had more questions than me."

"It all sounds very mysterious."

Emily clapped her hands together.

"What if you turn out to be a missing billionaire? When you remember, don't forget me."

"I doubt that'll be the case. If I had that kind of money, I'm sure my 'friends' would be swarming all around me."

Peters came back into the ward, Emily's parents following close behind.

"Emily. Your parents would like to say goodbye."

Emily got up and walked over to her parents. Her father glanced around the ward before settling his gaze on Taylor. When Peters showed people around, Taylor often felt like an animal on show in a zoo.

Peters was all charm and friendliness but did he have, as Emily had insinuated, another side? Taylor looked across at the two patients watching TV. Their eyes were glassy and vacant, registering nothing.

7

The queue of traffic snaked down the hill and was now over a mile long. Pritchard sat behind the wheel of his car, staring at the setting sun, which flickered through the trees on the horizon. He was annoyed, his thoughts flitting between Taylor's reappearance and the vexing subject of Jason Black's leaving party. The latter meant another evening wearing a fake smile, glad-handing and putting up with asinine conversation. Worst of all, it meant an evening with his wife. There were no tender feelings between the two of them, but, he thought, that was never the point of the marriage.

His phone rang, and he immediately pressed the button on the dashboard, diverting the call through to the car's speakers.

"Pritchard."

"Anne Richmond, sir."

"Well?"

"It's him, sir. ID is a positive."

For nearly thirty seconds, Pritchard remained silent.

"Sir?"

"Yes, erm, you're sure? It's really him?"

"Positive."

"And his head? The bump was there?"

"Yes."

Again, Pritchard fell deep into thought.

"Is the hospital safe?"

"It has all the usual security features. I don't see any immediate risk."

Anne ran through a detailed account of what she had seen.

"Did you get a chance to talk with him—*alone*?"

"Yes. He doesn't remember anything—other than the phrases Clean Start and Stonebridge."

"And this Dr Peters?"

"He seems genuine enough. He's been treating him since his admission. He runs the place and has free rein to do what he wants. If he was hostile, he would have had plenty of opportunities to act by now."

"I see. OK. Write up the report and put it on my desk before you go home."

Pritchard rang off. Jason Black no longer existed in his mind. One recurring phrase reverberated like a beating drum in his head: ID is a positive.

"Impossible," he muttered. "Impossible."

The beeping of a car horn brought him back to the present. He pressed down on the pedal, and his car edged forward.

It was a long hour before Pritchard reached the street where he lived. To his annoyance, all the parking bays were packed solid, most people preferring to stay in on this cold, miserable evening. So, he spent another ten minutes driving around the narrow residential streets, searching for a place to park. After finding an empty parking bay two roads away, he trudged back to his small terraced house. He could have afforded a more luxurious abode in the countryside, but he was a frugal man and, in any case, as far as he was concerned, a house was simply a place to eat and sleep.

Stepping in a puddle, he scowled as stagnant water splashed over his trousers and soaked his socks, exacerbating his irritability after the long drive. He just wanted to take a shower and get into some clean clothes. He pushed back the wrought-iron front gate that led to the small front garden. In the corner of his eye, he saw the glint of something metallic and spun around.

Sitting in a car across the road from him was a man wearing steel-rimmed glasses. He was leaning back in his seat, trying to conceal himself in the shadows cast by the streetlights. Realising that he had been seen, he started the engine, gunned down on the throttle and sped off. Pritchard watched the car until it was lost from sight.

He turned back to his house. The curtains were drawn, but the light was on in the living room, and he could see the silhouette of his svelte wife sitting on the sofa. He unlocked the front door and stepped into the hallway. The house was cold. She hasn't even bothered to put the heating on, he thought, with rising anger.

Melissa came out of the living room and stood in the hallway, a tumbler in one hand, a cigarette in the other. In the half-light from the living room, she looked more ferocious than ever. Without her makeup, her face was harsh, dark circles of fatigue and tension beneath her eyes.

"I don't suppose you've made dinner?" Pritchard said.

"What do you think? I only got here myself half an hour ago."

Pritchard said nothing and took off his overcoat.

"Is there any way to get out of this party?" Melissa asked.

Pritchard hung up his overcoat.

"No. It's important. All the top brass will be there. We have to make a good impression."

"I need another drink."

Melissa stormed back into the living room.

Pritchard looked down at the damp patch of carpet on which he stood, let out a sigh and followed her in. She was sitting on the sofa, her hand shaking as she poured vodka into her tumbler. To Pritchard's horror, the bottle was already half empty.

"You've had enough," he said, grabbing the bottle, the half-full tumbler falling to the floor.

Melissa sprang to her feet, and Pritchard grabbed her as she struggled to retrieve the bottle. He lashed out and slapped her hard across the face. She crumpled down on the sofa, holding her face, a red streak beginning to rise on her cheek. She looked up at him with a cold, inimical stare.

"You disgust me!" Pritchard said, his eyes smouldering.

"I wonder what your important top brass would think if they knew you hit your wife. I don't think that would do a lot for your precious career."

"Go ahead and tell them. I won't stop you."

Melissa stared down at the floor. Pritchard's lips curled up in a cruel smile. Yes, he was the one in control. The thought lifted his spirits.

"Stop feeling sorry for yourself," he said. "We both know the score. They're expecting us tonight, the picture of the happily married couple, and that's exactly what we're going to be."

8

A week earlier, Peters had told Taylor that, at any moment, all his memories could come flooding back. He had seen it happen with one of his patients a couple of years ago. It would be as if a light would suddenly be shone on everything hidden by the darkness, and he would see everything, even the things he may have wanted to forget.

The patient, Peters told him, had simply picked up his life from where he had left off. Would *he* be able to do that? What if he was not ready to deal with what he may discover about himself? What if he *had* been a monster? Peters didn't know anything about him, and neither did his sister. She had looked at him with such a strange expression when they had been alone. What did it mean? Was she concealing some horrible truth from him?

Peters had warned him that paranoia was a real possibility for someone with amnesia. He would have to trust people; this would be a vital part of his recovery. Peters was trying to help him, but maybe he was instead leading him to some unseen precipice.

Taylor's thoughts turned to Emily. He had only spoken to her for a few minutes but felt there was a connection between the two of them. Those few minutes had left an indelible impression upon him. She had a melancholy demeanour, which drew him closer to her and made her easy to trust. Something was stirring in the depths of her mind, upsetting her. She, too, was lonely. Loneliness often brought people together.

Her friendship meant an inordinate amount to him. Had he had so little in his life? The more he questioned who he was, the more afraid he became. He should start afresh. There was truth in what Emily had said; he would be spared having to deal with the emotional baggage of life that all people his age must have acquired.

Professor Belakovsky's soft voice broke Taylor from his thoughts. He had finished reading Peters' notes and took a small torch from the breast pocket of his jacket.

"I want to check to see that there's no pressure behind the eyes. Just look straight ahead for me."

Belakovsky shone the light in Taylor's eye, his pupil immediately contracting.

"Look up, to your left …"

A few seconds later, Belakovsky snapped off the torch and put it back in his pocket.

"It all looks fine. It's important that we don't rush things. Let them come back naturally."

"I understand, doctor. It's just so frustrating."

Belakovsky stroked his thick black moustache and said, "I know, my boy. You mustn't let yourself get depressed about it. Yours is not a simple problem, but I'm sure we'll get to the truth of who you are. Have faith."

"Will I simply be able to talk myself better?"

"That depends on whether or not there's physical damage. Let us consider what we do know."

Belakovsky sat down. His soft brown eyes stared out from his wrinkled, old face.

Smiling sympathetically, he said, "You've suffered minor physical trauma to your head—cuts and bruises. These are consistent with your fight in the high street. They could be masking pre-existing injuries and even internal damage to the brain. I've arranged for an MRI scan in a couple of days. Have you had any blackouts or seizures over the past week?"

"No. Right now, I've never felt better. If the problem's with my brain, what kind of things are we talking about?"

"Quite a few. At one end of the spectrum, your memory loss could simply be a result of a severe concussion. On the other, it could be a tumour. There've been many cases in which brain tumours can cause behavioural changes."

"And if that is the problem?"

"It's surgically removed. In most cases, the tumour is benign. It's the pressure it puts on the frontal lobe which causes behavioural changes and memory impairment. We would have to check that part of the brain every few years for signs of regrowth, but I would expect a full recovery. However, this is on the extreme end of the spectrum."

"So, it could all be physical, not psychiatric?"

"Yes."

Belakovsky cleared his throat.

"Let's put together what we do know. You were found dishevelled and disorientated, having awoken on a park bench. Dr Peters hasn't put out any publicity about your case, but your sister did find out that you were here from a friend who works for a local newspaper."

Belakovsky's eyes became flinty.

"Was she able to help you remember anything?"

"No, nothing."

"I see. She doesn't seem to have told Dr Peters much either. All we can be sure of are your feelings. You've experienced mild depression, anxiety and a sense of isolation. These are all common amongst amnesiacs, but we must determine which—if any—existed before."

"You think I could have been depressed, and this led to my amnesia?"

"A pre-existing mental condition cannot be ruled out. This is often the basis of a dissociative fugue. This is when a person creates a whole new identity for themselves. Usually, it involves leaving one's old life and starting afresh someplace new. It may be that you were unhappy with your life and tried to escape from it. But something went wrong, and instead of immersing yourself in your new identity, you've been left in limbo, inbetween identities, with only partial memories."

"So, even if you can cure me, I may still be ill—depressed and afraid."

"Depressed, maybe, but fear is a symptom, not an illness. I'm sure those feelings will not persist once we get to the truth of who you are."

"So, all these thoughts about being a secret agent may just be part of some fantasy that I created to escape my real life?"

"Possibly, but there may be an element of truth in them."

Taylor looked carefully, very carefully at Belakovsky.

"You really think so?"

"One thing I've learnt from my years in psychiatry is never to rule anything out. It may seem a bit far-fetched, but that doesn't preclude the possibility. According to the notes that I've read, you don't have any concrete reason for believing you were an agent."

"No, it's a vague feeling that keeps coming up."

"If we do go along the lines that you are experiencing a fugue, it may be that you did work for the secret service but not as a spy. There are many other roles you could have had: admin staff, a contact, informant or some other minor role. The fugue may have been triggered because you were fed up with your job and *wanted* to be a spy."

Belakovsky took a sheet of paper from the desk and said, "Let's talk about Clean Start and Stonebridge. Do you have any idea what they mean?"

"No."

"If not memories, do they elicit any emotions?"

"No. They're just words. They mean nothing to me. Do *you* know what they mean?"

"Yes, and this is why I don't entirely discount the possibility that you worked for the secret service.

"It won't do any harm telling you. About three years ago, an Australian Industrialist, Carl Brenner, suspected of spying for the Russians, managed to leave the country before the security services could arrest him. He lived in an Oxfordshire mansion called Stonebridge. Does any of this sound familiar?"

"No."

"The innocent and I suppose obvious explanation is that you saw this on the news or read it in a newspaper, and it got stored in your subconscious."

"But why would I remember it?"

Belakovsky smiled.

"There're no reasons for a lot of the things we remember. It was a random memory that may have just gained undue prominence. It may be that you simply incorporated it in your fugue, or as I said, you may have been working for the secret service."

"But if I am—"

"I've made enquiries."

"And?"

"Patience, my boy. Patience. These things take time."

"And Clean Start?"

"That … I don't know what it means. Hopefully, that will come back to you in time. You're sure you don't have any memory at all about what it could be?"

"None."

"Oh, well. There may come a point when we have to force matters, but we're a long way from that. Once you completely settle down into a routine, things will start to come back."

"Dr Peters spoke very highly of you. I'm sure if anyone can help me, it's—"

"Tut-tut. Reputations count for nothing. I'll be judged on how well you recover."

"Even if I can't remember who I was, I don't want to be afraid anymore."

"In time, the fear will pass. As I said, don't try to force things. Be patient, my boy. Be patient."

9

Soothing orchestral music filled the day room in which several patients watched TV and played board games while a nurse wheeled around a trolley and dispensed medication.

Emily sat alone at a table, absently shuffling the pieces of a jigsaw. It was a five-thousand-piece puzzle of Constable's *Hay-Wain*, which would cover the entire table when completed. She had successfully pieced together a small section of the trees, but the sky was a daunting prospect. She had half an eye on Dr Campbell's office in which Belakovsky was treating Taylor.

A sudden clatter of hail against a windowpane drew her attention. The sky was dark, the branches of a tree swaying in a sudden gust of wind. She let out an exaggerated shudder. It was good to be inside in the warmth of the hospital.

Taylor emerged from Dr Campbell's office. On seeing Emily, her back to him, he was momentarily unsure whether he should go up and talk with her. An odd sense of propriety came over him, and he did not want to appear presumptuous.

Also, Belakovsky's suggestion that he really could have been a spy had unsettled him. There could be a lot more to his past than he had imagined, and he didn't want to draw her into a dark and dangerous world.

However, he put aside his fears. A selfish desire to be near her, draw her out and get to know her better prevailed. Right now, he needed friendship. She turned when she heard the sound of his approaching footsteps.

"Is it hard?" Taylor asked, picking up a piece of the puzzle.

"Impossible," Emily said, pushing the pieces away. "I think you just have to get lucky with the sky. There's too much cloud, and it all looks the same."

Taylor sat down across from her.

"How was your talk with Belakovsky?"

"He arranged for me to have a scan in a couple of days. He wants to be sure there's no physical damage."

"You seem a bit down."

Taylor nodded. He had hoped for so much more from the great Belakovsky, but it seemed just a continuation of Peters' talking cure.

"He said I should be patient."

"So, you still haven't been able to remember anything?"

"I remember some things."

Emily waited expectantly.

"Things from when I was very young."

"That's a start."

"I suppose, but they're memories that don't have anything to do with me as a man. I remember my parents, my dog, I ..."

Taylor broke off, his face wrinkled in concentration.

"What is it?"

"I don't remember having a sister."

"Oh?"

"Nothing at all. I remember birthday parties and trips to museums and zoos, but there's no sister in any of those."

"You may have had a bad experience, and you're blocking her out."

"It could be."

"You've got to think of the positives. At least you're starting to remember."

"But all the things I remember haven't made me any happier. I think I was a constant worrier. I don't think I was ever very happy. I remember when I was eleven. I was in the school playground. We had a small garden in the school, and I'd been let out of my regular lesson to dig up the weeds and plant some seeds. I remember looking out past the fence that ran around the school and being afraid that I would soon have to leave and go to high school. I would have to make new friends and start all over. It's how I feel now. I feel like I've been afraid all my life. It's in my genes, my DNA. It's what makes me who I am. Maybe that's what I've been trying to escape from—this constant living in fear. Belakovsky asked me about …"

Taylor checked himself.

"Yes?" Emily said.

"I've been having a delusion. At least that's what Peters thinks it is—Belakovsky isn't so sure. This is hard to talk about without sounding crazy."

"I wouldn't worry about that. *I'm* not the sanest person in the world. I won't judge you."

"I didn't mean that. I …"

"I know. I know."

It was strange, Taylor thought, how talking to this girl made everything so much easier and more so than talking to Belakovsky or Peters.

"I keep having this thought in my head that I used to be some kind of government agent. A spy."

Emily clapped her hands together.

"That's so much better than my billionaire idea."

"You think it could be true?"

"Why not? You could've been a spy. It would explain why you told me your name was Taylor."

Taylor wrinkled his brow.

Emily said, "When you ask most people their name, they give their first name. You didn't."

"I didn't realise that. But there must be a lot of jobs where people use their last name."

"Not as many as you'd think. I know they do that in the army and police. We should make a list. What else did you talk about?"

"Stonebridge."

"What's that?"

Taylor recounted Belakovsky's explanation and asked, "Do you remember it?"

"Three years ago, I was in high school, going out with Bobby Durant and listening to Lady Gaga's *Poker Face*. I didn't pay attention to the news. But it would be exciting if you were involved in all that."

"It could all just be a fantasy. Belakovsky thought it might've been part of a delusion—a fugue is what he called it—where I tried to escape from an unhappy past."

Taylor's face became dark.

"What if I never remember who I am?"

"Does it matter?"

Taylor looked at Emily in surprise and said, "Everyone needs to know who they are. If I don't, I'll always go through life wondering."

"That might not be a bad thing."

"How do you mean?"

"If you had a particularly unhappy past, you've got a chance to start again. Not many people get that kind of opportunity."

Taylor shook his head and said, "A person's still responsible for all the things they've done in their life."

"I'm sure your sister will be able to tell you what kind of a man you were."

"I don't think we were that close. I seem to have been the kind of man who kept a lot of secrets."

Taylor's face registered a surge of agitated emotion.

"If only I could remember."

"You'll never will if you get stressed. Let's try and finish this."

Taylor picked up a piece and said, "It's a bit like my mind, all in pieces waiting for someone to put it back together and make sense of it."

He smiled and added, "At least we can be sure of one thing, I wasn't a writer. I'd never sell any books writing stuff like that. How was your session with Peters?"

"That's not till tomorrow."

10

Anne put down the phone and stared out of the window. It was five-thirty and already dark. There was a steady stream of cars heading out of the car park to join the evening rush hour traffic that was already clogging up the perimeter road. Turning back to her computer screen, she checked the details of her report one last time.

There was, she thought, something to be envied about a man who was not bound by the past. Although not knowing the past meant he might be condemned to make the same mistakes over again. Better that than to be held prisoner by them. She had not been briefed about who Taylor was, but, from meeting him, she knew he was a lonely, unhappy man. Whatever his past, he was free of it. He had the prospect of an untainted future ahead of him.

Satisfied that there was nothing else to add and that she had not omitted anything, Anne saved her report, pushed the keyboard away and fell back in her chair. It had been a long, tiring day but an interesting one. It had been good to get out and do something physical.

Around her, other workers were putting on coats and getting ready for an evening out. A girl let out a shrill laugh as a colleague grabbed her around the waist.

"Cut it out, Harry," she said giggling, guiltily glancing around, conscious of having disturbed some of the more conscientious staff.

Anne looked at the couple with a trace of envy. Why was it that she could get no enjoyment from life? There had been a time when going out for drinks after work had been such fun.

The light, casual conversation and laughter that had once filled those hours before returning home now only left her feeling empty and alone. A part of her still yearned for human company, but the price of a night out was remorseless guilt.

She got up and gathered up her coat that was slung over the backrest of her chair. As she did so, Tom Sutherland came into the office, looked around and, seeing Anne, waved. He picked his way between the desks.

He was young, clean-shaven, still carrying baby fat around his chubby cheeks. He was straight out of university and at a stage in his career when everything was still exciting, and he felt his life was at the start of a big adventure.

"I came by at lunchtime," he said. "Sarah told me you hadn't come in."

"I had to go out."

"All day?"

"Yes, I got back an hour ago."

"Anything interesting?"

"I can't tell you."

One of the advantages of working for GCHQ was that you could openly tell people you couldn't or didn't want to talk about work without offending them.

"Have you got any plans for tonight?" Tom asked. "I thought, maybe, we could have a drink … dinner?"

Anne was torn. She wanted to go home. But what was home? An empty flat full of memories of a life that had been so cruelly taken from her.

Tom was such a straightforward boy, and he was obviously keen on her. He had only been with GCHQ for a few months and knew nothing about her past. But then, no one did. Anne had no close friends or confidants. Her past resided only in her mind and the files kept in Human Resources. She was good at concealing her emotions. She had changed this past year but only on the inside. Outwardly she showed no trace of what had happened. She wanted to move on and fall in love again, but she backed away from doing so whenever the possibility arose.

"In the canteen?" she asked.

"I thought we could go somewhere in town. There's a new place that's just opened on Blenheim Street."

Tom looked hopefully at Anne, and she relented.

"OK," she said.

Tom smiled and said, "Great. I'll meet you there at seven. Let me give you my number."

They walked down to the car park together, and Anne waved at Tom's car as he drove off. She looked up at the Doughnut and its brightly lit corridors. The biting cold wind cut across her face. She got into her car, drove off, and joined the short queue of cars at the barrier.

Anne's flat was a government subsidised development that housed professionals—mostly single women like herself. She took the stairs to the second floor. Unlocking the front door, she stepped into the living room. It was decorated neutrally and comprised of a three-piece suite, flatscreen TV, and thick beige carpet. She stood, deep in thought. The flat had not changed in over a year. Nothing had been added or taken away. It was a permanent shrine to his memory and exactly the way it had been a year ago when she had received the fateful phone call. I'm only twenty-eight, and I'm turning into Miss Havisham, she thought. The feeble attempt at levity only unsettled her; there was a frightening element of truth in it. She took off her coat, threw it on the sofa and went into the kitchen.

Opening the fridge, she automatically selected one of several ready meals stacked on the shelf and a bottle of wine from the rack. After piercing the meal's plastic sleeve with a fork, she put it into the microwave. She then uncorked the wine and poured herself a generous measure. While the microwave heated the bland meal, occasionally making a popping sound, she took several gulps of her wine.

What am I doing? she thought. I can't live like this. She pulled open the microwave's door, grabbed the meal. The plastic tray was scorching hot, and she immediately dropped it onto the floor. Going over to the sink, she ran cold water over her hand until it no longer smarted, and then grabbed a tea towel, gingerly picked up the meal and threw it in the bin.

I'm going out to have dinner with Tom, she decided. She finished off her glass of wine, went into the bedroom, kicked off her shoes, pulled open a drawer and took out a black blouse. She froze, staring at it, a pained expression on her face. She let it slip from her hands onto the floor and glanced across at the wardrobe in the corner. She went over to it, flung open its doors and stared at the row of clothes.

She took a wool coat from the rack and went back and sat on the bed, holding the coat close to her face, the soft wool rubbing against her cheek. It had been his favourite coat. There had been a time when she could still smell him on it, but now that smell only lived in her mind. There was a loose thread on the sleeve. She tugged at it, and it came away in her hand. He had worn it the whole winter they had first met.

There was no escaping him. If she was not thinking about him during the day, she dreamt about him at night. She dreamt of the little things: coffee in Gordon Square, riding the tube together to work and dodging showers on a night out in the West

End. The happier the dream, the more bitter she felt when she awoke. But she could not help herself; she wanted to think back to those happy times whenever she had the chance, even if it did leave her feeling wretched afterwards. She pulled back her sleeve. It was six-thirty. She took out her phone, tapped out a message and pressed send. She hoped Tom would not take it badly.

11

"All very atmospheric," Sir Raymond Charters said, taking a healthy sip from his champagne and cognac aperitif.

He was an unapologetic sensualist. For him, life was a game, not dissimilar from when he had stood, nearly forty years earlier, on the playing fields of Eton, discussing with his friends how he would run the country when he was elected Prime Minister. Although that ambition had never come to fruition, he was not bitter. After all, things had not worked out badly; he was Director of GCHQ. There wasn't a hostile fibre in his body.

He cast a beady eye over the conference room, which had been transformed into a plush banquet hall for the evening. Running along almost the entire length of the room was a thirty-seat table draped in a blood-red damask tablecloth. It looked magnificent: napkins folded Dutch bonnet style, a cluster of twelve candles on each of the seven candelabras, standing on mirror plateaus, and cutlery that glinted in the flickering candlelight. Several comfortable burgundy sofas and armchairs were scattered around the periphery of the room, small cliques of staff standing around them, mingling, the murmur of chatter filling the room.

Charters said, "I was hoping it would be something low-key—something more intimate. You know, I had considered having it at my place. Agnes loves to play the hostess, but she's got the wretched flu."

Anderson, standing beside Charters, immaculate in his dinner jacket, nodded in agreement and said, "I just hope that by the end of the evening, it doesn't get too boisterous. Some of these youngsters already look a bit worse for wear."

"It's an open bar, Lyle. You can't blame them. Youth is meant to be enjoyed. It'll only be a blink of an eye before they'll be old duffers like us, having to down their Chardonnays with a handful of statins.

"I'm glad you took up my invitation to come. I thought with this Taylor business still unresolved that you might not be able to fit it in. The situation's contained?"

"I think so. Lewis sent someone to verify his identity."

"Oh? Who?"

"Anne Richmond. She used to be with us but transferred a year ago. He's got doubts about whether it's Taylor."

"Did he give a reason?"

"He doesn't think someone can just disappear like that without a trace—and for what purpose?"

"What about you? What do you think?"

"I hope it's him."

"Why?"

"The alternative is that someone knows about Clean Start."

"Yes, I see your point."

"We'll know for sure when Richmond reports back. If it's him, we'll extract him."

"You're happy to wait until then."

"Lewis wants to play it slowly."

"And you're on board with that?"

"We don't want to rouse any suspicions. If anyone else has eyes on him, they won't want to act unless they're sure. If we storm in, it'll be a signal that he *is* Taylor."

"I see."

"I know that Stonebridge was a major setback. We'll do all we can to stop this getting ugly."

"Keep a lid on it. That's all I'm asking. Ah, here's Lewis."

Pritchard and Melissa walked through the doorway. Pritchard had all the confidence of a man walking into an important function with arguably the most beautiful woman on his arm. At times like this, he appreciated her worth to him.

Anderson found himself admiring Melissa; she had such poise and grace, her elegant blue gown flowing around her heels.

Pritchard and Melissa came straight up to Charters and Anderson. Charters immediately addressed himself to Melissa. It was no secret that he was partial to a beautiful woman.

Taking her hand and kissing it, he said, "You look magnificent, my dear."

"You're too kind, Sir Raymond."

"Not at all."

Pritchard looked on approvingly. It was a marvel how Melissa had transformed herself from the wretched woman he had thrown down on the sofa. With a thin veneer of makeup expertly applied, her skin looked flawless, with no sign of the slight bruise on her cheek.

Pritchard said, "Very impressive. You wouldn't know it for the conference room."

Charters turned to him.

"Yes," he said, taking two balloon wine glasses from a waitress's silver tray and handing them to Pritchard and Melissa.

Melissa took a sip.

"That's delicious," she said.

Anderson's wife, Margaret, joined the group. She wore a green evening gown. She had applied a tad too much makeup, and her face looked a bit artificial.

"Melissa, it's been too long," she said. "We've got so much to catch up on. We should leave the boys alone. You know how they always talk shop."

Margaret took Melissa by the hand.

Charters was about to protest when Margaret cut him short.

"No, Raymond. We girls have got things we need to catch up on."

"But—"

"No, she's coming with me."

Melissa, smiling coquettishly, said, "I'm sorry, Sir Raymond."

Charters chuckled and said, "Very well. Beauty has its privileges."

Margaret led Melissa away.

Admiring the two women, Charters said, "Longevity is the least of nature's gifts,"

"What's that?" Anderson said.

"Juvenal, the Roman poet. To be young and have your whole life ahead of you."

"We're not that old."

"Have you looked in the mirror lately?"

Charters turned to Pritchard and said, "Talking of looks, Lewis. You're a genius to have snapped up such a beautiful wife."

"Yes," Pritchard said. "She looks very nice tonight."

"Nice! Nice doesn't do justice to her. She's a goddess. Ah, she's wasted on you."

Pritchard wondered whether Charters, who had done his fair share of philandering, was insinuating anything.

"Have you met Jason Black?" Charters said.

"No," Pritchard said.

"He's quite the character. Although, there were a few rumours about him a while back."

"He's married now," Anderson said.

"That doesn't mean anything," Charters said. "A lot of queers get married."

Anderson raised an eyebrow.

"I understand it's OK to call them that," Charters said. "They use it amongst themselves. These things come and go in cycles."

"Is it still deemed a security risk?" Anderson asked.

"Being queer? Not really. There's a whole bunch of them in the cabinet. It's like a gay mafia."

"But nothing was ever proven against Black."

"No. Don't get me wrong; I like the man, even if he is queer. You remember the time we went to that Indian wedding for one of his friends. The one where the groom wore those robes and turban?"

"The Sikh wedding."

"Yes, that was it."

Charters turned to Pritchard and said, "They wanted the two of us to take part and had us walking around and saying things we didn't understand. At one point, I thought Lyle and I had got married."

"For all I know, we are," Anderson said, chuckling.

The two men laughed. Pritchard joined in.

Charters said, "I suppose in a few years, no one will bat an eyelid about all these queers getting married."

Charters scrutinised Pritchard, who stood stiffly, taking occasional sips from his glass, and said, "It's like old Monty said, a charter for buggery. Don't you agree, Lewis?"

"I suppose you could see it that way."

"Come now. You're amongst friends. There's no need to hold back. No one's saying *you're* a ponce—a queer, I mean."

"I've never really given it much thought."

Charters turned away, not hiding his disappointment in the response. An awkward silence fell over the group. Pritchard stared down into his glass.

What was the matter with him? Over the years, he had developed a skill for small talk, but this evening it had already deserted him. He had been given one opportunity to say something witty, and he had fallen flat on his face.

Taylor's reappearance had thrown him off balance. The tone of the conversation had also become quite ugly, and he could not think of a way to lighten it.

Stumbling about in his mind for something to say, he said, "I got the report back on Taylor. It's—"

Raising a hand, Charters said, "Let's not talk shop."

"I'm sorry, sir."

Pritchard clamped his jaws shut morosely. He could not help the colour rising on his face. He looked across the room and caught a flash of a malicious smile on Melissa's face. She was enjoying his discomfort. She turned away and resumed her conversation with Margaret.

Pritchard glanced around the room at the groups of people. They were all having such a good time, lost in the moment. He felt miserable.

In these opulent surroundings, he should have felt the same sense of achievement he had when he had taken a moment that morning to look up at the Doughnut. But he did not. As a child, he had despised his life: the cold, dank council flat, a drunken father and defeated mother, downtrodden and full of despair—both sent to an early grave worrying about debts and bills. That had been real life. Everyone here had had a privileged upbringing; there was no one to whom he could relate. He would always be the outsider.

Charters and Anderson were greeting a new arrival whom Pritchard did not know. One of the ambitious young generation who would undoubtedly be eyeing his position in a few years, Pritchard mused. He absently strolled around the room. He felt awkward and didn't want to talk to anyone. People glanced at him. Did they even know who he was, he wondered? He stopped by the banquet table.

Anderson joined him and said, "That's Wheeler."

Both men looked at Wheeler, who was talking to a small, shrivelled up balding man with gapped, yellow teeth and a pallid complexion. In contrast, Wheeler had a Hollywood smile, a lustrous mane of jet-black hair and a thick, determined jaw.

Anderson said, "Have you met him?"

"No."

"He's the new big thing in H Branch. He's got a lot of fresh ideas. He took over after old Braintree died."

Once again, bile welled up in Pritchard's chest. He remembered how, as a young recruit, he had put forward so many bright ideas. They had all been lost in the ether, or some toff higher up had passed them off as their own.

Anderson said, "But he's quite the bore. He likes to think of himself as a raconteur. He's one of those people who's done everything—twice."

Wheeler walked up to the banquet table and surreptitiously took a name card from it.

"What's he doing?" Pritchard asked.

"It's a game. You take a friend's name card, write something witty or embarrassing on it. At the end of the evening, when the director's making his toasts, he reads out what's been written on them."

Charters joined the pair and said, "Have you met the man of the hour?"

Beside him, the lean, athletic figure of Jason Black. If anything, his face was too smooth, his skin too clear. Pritchard resented the fact that Black's face had not been prematurely aged like his own due to a constant need to be on his guard.

"It's more than I deserve," Black said.

"Not at all," Charters said. "You earned it."

Pritchard thought, no matter what he said or did, he would never be one of them. They had their secret ways and were a closed society. Everything he had said this evening felt jarring and like a faux pas. He glanced across the room.

Wheeler was no more than thirty and already heading his own division. His youth perturbed Pritchard. Had he not been told who he was, it would never have occurred to him that Wheeler was someone of importance. This lack of clear distinctions was another reason why he loathed these occasions. Without the assured public-school handshake and easy smile, he had, no doubt, by some of those present, been mistaken for a menial functionary.

As Anderson drove home, he glanced across at Margaret. In his eyes, she looked magnificent—she always did. Her wild youth behind her, she had adopted a health-conscious outlook on life, based on the much-touted mindfulness approach. It had done wonders for her complexion.

Anderson said, "Did you have a good time, dear?"

Margaret shrugged.

"So-so. It wasn't as good as last year's bash for Waverley, but it was good to see some new faces."

"Something's on your mind?"

"Yes. Melissa."

"What about her? She looked radiant."

"Yes, she did."

"Then, what is it?"

"I can't believe that she's still with Lewis."

"I've never seen the attraction myself."

"That's because you're a man; you only operate on one level. No, it's more than that."

"Did she say anything to you?"

"No. We chatted, but she kept her cards close to her chest. There's no light in those eyes. She's got a lovely smile, but the eyes are the giveaway."

"You're reading too much into things. They've been married a long time."

"Not that long. Only three years. It was straight after all that fuss about Stonebridge."

"Oh, yes."

"You don't have an eye for these things. Like most men, you only see the surface, not what lies beneath. That's where the real interest is. No, trust me, dear. I can tell when there's no chemistry. It's as if it's all one big act."

"All couples have difficulties."

"True, but this is more than a little difficulty. The way she looked at him this evening. It's as if she positively hates him."

12

Golden sunlight seeped in through the curtains into Taylor's room. He slowly opened his eyes and yawned. It had been the first night since his admission that he had had an unbroken sleep.

This morning, he felt refreshed and peaceful. He had dreamt about Emily. The details of his past may still have been a mystery, but he did not feel despondent. She was a balm for all the suffering suppressed in his subconscious. With her, there seemed a possibility of a happy future.

The door opened and a burly male nurse, wearing a white tunic, entered.

"You up. Good," he said gruffly, in a thick Slavic accent.

"Morning," Taylor answered, yawning again. "Where's Alice?"

"It her day off."

He put a thimble-sized paper cup on Taylor's nightstand.

"You take these."

Up close, the nurse was a particularly unattractive man with thick eyebrows, a large nose and a Neanderthal sloped forehead.

Taylor picked up the paper cup. The two small pills rattled inside.

"What are these?"

"For the scan."

"That's today?"

"Yes."

"Belakovsky said it would be tomorrow."

"He change it," the nurse said, watching Taylor with animal cunning through narrowed eyes.

Taylor swallowed the pills, washing them down with a glass of water. They left a bitter taste in his mouth. He put the glass back down on the nightstand.

"Good," the nurse said,

He left the room and returned a few moments later, pushing a squeaky wheelchair.

"I'm OK to walk," Taylor said.

Abruptly, he fell back in his bed. All of a sudden, he had become listless, and his vision blurry. He closed his eyes. The nurse walked over to him and pulled up his eyelid.

"Good. It make it easy for you. You not feel anything this way."

Taylor, his mouth numb, tried to speak but was unable. Mustering all his strength, he threw a punch, hitting the nurse square on the jaw. The nurse fell to the floor, taking the nightstand crashing down with him. He immediately scrambled back to his feet and was about to retaliate when a voice called out.

"Don't mark him!"

The nurse turned to a female nurse, with a harsh, masculine face, wearing a green surgical gown, who stood in the doorway.

In a clipped foreign accent, she added, "He's waiting. Hurry up."

She went back out into the corridor.

The nurse turned to Taylor and snarled.

"You regret that," he said.

Taylor stared blankly at him. The drugs had worked through his system, and he was now paralysed, his face frozen. The nurse hauled him off the bed and put him in the wheelchair. Taking no chances, he fastened Taylor's forearms, using leather straps, to the armrest. His feet were similarly secured to the footrests before he was wheeled out of the room.

Taylor's head fell to one side. Life in the ward was carrying on as usual. Nurses were doing their rounds, administering medication, and patients sat watching TV and playing board games. He did not see Emily.

He looked up at the nurse with mute appeal. But the nurse stared fixedly ahead, perspiration breaking out on his forehead, breathing heavily as he pushed the wheelchair down the corridor.

After passing through several corridors, Taylor was pushed into a small operating theatre with a table at its centre, above it spotlights blazing, momentarily blinding him. Belakovsky emerged from a small side room, drying his hands. The female nurse, now wearing a face mask, handed him a pair of nitrile gloves which he put on.

Belakovsky said, "It's a pity it has to end this way, my boy. Lobotomies aren't as routine as they once were, but I've done a great many in Moscow. It won't hurt. There'll be no more being lonely and afraid."

He turned to the female nurse and said a few words in Russian. She nodded and left the room. He turned to the male nurse, who was standing behind the wheelchair.

"Put him on the table," Belakovsky ordered.

The nurse unstrapped Taylor's arms and feet and lifted him onto the table. Belakovsky proceeded to examine the surgical instruments laid out on a tray that glinted under the bright spotlights.

Why? Taylor thought. Why is Belakovsky doing this? It made no sense at all. Unless he really was a spy, someone of importance. But whatever the reason, he had to get out. He felt numb inside, trying to think of a way of escape but knowing that there wasn't any. He clenched his eyes and felt a tear trickle down his cheek. He tried to speak but could only utter meaningless groans.

Although he was in no condition for deep philosophical reflections, he did begin to speculate on the possible life he had lived. If this was indeed the end, he felt no bitterness or anger. What was there to be bitter about? His mind drifted from one delirious thought to another. This was not a moment for recriminations. There were failures in every man's life, and no doubt, he had had his fair share, but there must have been successes along the way too, even if he could not remember them. If he had regrets, he was spared the knowledge of what they were. All he did know was that he had feelings for Emily. He would give anything for one last chance to tell her how he felt about her—to tell her that he loved her.

He looked over at Belakovsky, who stood, nodding, mentally preparing himself for the operation.

Suddenly, Belakovsky glanced up and looked at the door, his eyes narrow with tension.

"She's taking too long!" he said.

The male nurse turned to the door. Just then, it opened, and the female nurse entered. Her gown was creased and ruffled; her hair tousled.

"What took you so long?" Belakovsky said. "Never mind. We have to hurry. Prepare him."

The female nurse took two surgical wipes from the tray and proceeded to wipe Taylor's forehead. He felt nothing, staring ahead at the nurse. She was intent on her job and didn't look him in the eyes.

"That's enough," Belakovsky said.

The nurse stepped aside, allowing Belakovsky to take up his position. Taylor's eyes darted about the room. The male nurse was standing on the other side of the table, tensely licking his lips.

"Scalpel," Belakovsky said, holding out his hand.

The female nurse took the scalpel from the tray. In one swift movement, she lunged at the male nurse, impaling the blade in his throat. His guttural shriek was immediately cut short as his vocal cord was completely severed, sending a jet of blood gushing out. He reached up and grabbed his throat, his mouth gaping foolishly. Blood spewed out from between his fingers, and the colour drained from his face as he collapsed to the floor.

The female nurse turned to Belakovsky, who instinctively grabbed a scalpel from the tray. The nurse stepped towards him. Belakovsky, the features of his face twisting wildly, backed away into a corner.

"What are you doing?" he said. "Have you gone mad?"

Emily removed her mask and threw it onto the floor.

Belakovsky glanced at the open door. Emily took a step toward it, cutting off any possible escape route. Belakovsky smiled, and his face relaxed.

"We always take what steps are necessary," he said.

He raised his scalpel to his throat and expertly sliced his carotid artery.

13

Peters cut a dejected figure, sitting on a chair in his office. He hung his head and stared down at the floor, his mind in a loop, replaying the events of the previous hour.

He had been driving back to the hospital with Campbell when a black BMW flashed past.

Looking into the rearview mirror, he said, "Wasn't that Belakovsky's car?"

Campbell said, "I think so. It looks like he's in a rush."

"I thought …"

"What?"

"I thought that a girl was driving."

Chuckling, Campbell said, "You think he's got a girl on the go?"

Peters said nothing. He had such respect for Belakovsky that he wouldn't even joke about him in the privacy of his thoughts, let alone out loud.

They drove on in silence.

When they arrived at the hospital, all appeared to be as usual, but there was a space where Belakovsky's car had been parked that morning.

Campbell said, "Looks like it *was* him."

Peters said nothing. He felt it in his bones, a burgeoning sense that something was wrong. He got out of the car and rushed to the hospital's entrance, and threw open the doors.

The receptionist, almost hysterical, was talking on the phone, a nurse standing over her, wiping away tears. The two of them looked up as Peters stormed in.

"What's happened?" he said.

"Oh, doctor," the nurse said, her voice quivering.

Peters rushed up to her.

"What is it?" he demanded.

"Professor Belakovsky and two of the nurses have been murdered."

"Where are they?"

"In the surgery," the nurse said, snivelling.

Peters sprinted down the corridor. In less than a minute, he was standing outside the operating theatre. Through the doorway, he could see the legs of the prostrate male nurse. He tentatively walked up to the door. At its threshold, he slumped against the doorframe. Before him, the male nurse face down in a pool of blood. Behind the operating table lay Belakovsky's body.

The image of the dead Belakovsky would not leave Peters' mind for even a second. The academic community was a cruel one. He would be blamed and thought to be complicit in depriving it of one of its greatest thinkers. The truth of what had happened was incredible. Conspiracy theories would no doubt abound, and he would be a central protagonist in all of them. He would be guilty by association. All those doors which he had imagined would open were now firmly shut, probably forever.

DCI Karen Hall came into the office. She had seen reactions like Peters' many times before in her long career. She had given him half an hour to compose himself, and she could see that he would need a lot more time to recover. However, she could not wait any longer; it was vital to get the facts whilst they were still fresh in his mind.

Peters looked up.

"I can't believe it," he said.

Hall drew up a chair beside him.

"I know," she said. "Murder's a terrible thing."

"Have you found them yet?"

"Not yet."

"I suppose you want to ask me some questions."

"Do you think you're up to it?"

"Yes."

"Tell me about Bruce Taylor. What was he admitted for?"

"Amnesia."

"Was there any indication he was dangerous?"

"None! Of course, he did have that fight in Haylesbury, but if I hadn't been told about it, I would never have believed it. He was so placid and never raised his voice. He got on with everyone. He wanted help."

"A fight? Tell me about it."

"He'd been sleeping in the park. When he woke up, he was confused and ran into the back of some man, knocking him over. They got into a fight—more of a scuffle really—from what the police told me."

"The police came here?"

"Yes. They brought him here. Two of them."

Hall glanced up at her sergeant, who stood by the door, taking notes.

"Were they in uniform?"

"No. They wore suits."

"Did they show you ID?"

"Yes, badges and cards."

"Does this happen often?"

"The police coming here?"

"Yes."

"It's the first time."

"Why did they bring him here and not the hospital A&E?"

"Apart from being a bit scruffy, he didn't seem to be badly hurt. He only had a few cuts and bumps on his head, so he didn't need any emergency care. His mental health was a more obvious concern, and we're the closest specialist centre. Are you absolutely sure *he* murdered Belakovsky?"

"We're keeping an open mind, but it looks that way. Along with the girl, they're the only patients not accounted for. You saw the girl, Emily, driving Belakovsky's car."

"I'm not a hundred per cent sure it was her, but it was definitely a girl driving."

"Did these policemen give you any documentation or forms when they handed Taylor over?"

"No. They said they would send some later—after they had done their paperwork—but they never did."

"Tell me about Taylor."

"It was a straightforward case of amnesia. I've treated several patients with the condition. He didn't seem the type who would do something like this."

Inwardly, Hall sighed. She didn't think much of the framed diplomas plastered across the office wall. You were a good judge of character, or you weren't. It wasn't something that could be taught on some degree course. Peters had immediately struck her as being too trusting.

"He was *your* patient?"

"Yes, but I'd handed him over to Belakovsky. He was very interested in treating him."

"Oh, why the interest if it was just a straightforward case?"

"I don't know. I didn't ask. I was just astonished that he was coming here. He's a legend in the field of psychiatry."

"He spent time with Taylor?"

"They had one session yesterday evening."

"Alone?"

"Yes."

"Did Belakovsky discuss it with you?"

"No. We were going to go over things this morning while we did our rounds, but I got called away to a patient emergency. He might have written some notes and left them in the office.

"Dr Campbell's office?"

"Yes."

"What was he doing in the operating theatre?"

"I don't know. He had free rein as to what he did and where he went. You don't tell someone like Belakovsky what to do."

"Is it usual to operate on amnesiacs?"

"No, the theatre isn't used much. It's a relic from when this place used to be part of the main trust. The only time I can remember it being used was when a plumber, who was doing some work on the guttering, fell off his ladder. That was about a year ago. He broke his femur, and we operated on him here instead of taking him to the A&E."

"So, there's no reason you can think of why he was going to operate?"

"None. Taylor's case wasn't that urgent. However, Belakovsky might have discovered something during their session."

"How likely is that?"

"Not very. Not without a scan."

"Did Taylor have any visitors?"

"His sister came yesterday."

"Tell me about her."

"She was very ordinary—about the same age. We spoke about his life. She didn't seem to know much about him. I got the impression they'd drifted apart."

"How did she know he was here?"

"She has a friend who works at the *Gazette*."

"Do you have her contact details?"

"The sister? Yes, they're on the system. I can get them up for you—"

"Later. I've still got a few more questions. Tell me about this patient you were visiting this morning. It was a house call?"

"Yes, a false alarm. Just a case of delirium caused by dehydration. It's not uncommon in old people."

"How were you told about it?"

"I got a call from his GP."

"And that's normal?"

"Yeah, pretty much. It's either that or an email if it isn't urgent."

"And the GP missed this. I'm no expert, but I would've thought it was a pretty straightforward diagnosis."

"Yes, it was. It was obvious from the moment I saw him. I'll have to get back to him on this. It isn't good enough."

"The GP?"

"Yes."

"You've worked with him before?"

"No, he's a locum. I've forgotten his name—I jotted it down somewhere. He got called away on another case before I got there. He left a note. I'll have to get back to the surgery to find out who it was."

"What about Emily?"

"She was only admitted yesterday—came in with her parents. I was going to start her treatment today."

"What was wrong with her?"

"Anxiety."

"Serious enough to be admitted?"

"I didn't have a chance to make an assessment. From what her parents told me, she had all the classic signs of an imminent breakdown."

"And her parents? Anything unusual?"

"No. Pretty much as I would expect: middle-class, a bit stuffy."

Twenty minutes later, Hall concluded her interview. After Peters had been led away, she turned to her sergeant.

"Well?" she said.

The sergeant raised an eyebrow and flicked through the pages in his notepad.

"Three bodies, one of whom is a world-famous Russian psychiatrist and a suspect who's an amnesiac. We've got our work cut out on this one."

Hall's thoughts turned to Campbell, who was waiting in the next room. She would interview him next. A detective always had to keep an open mind, and there was a possibility that Peters and Campbell could have been involved somehow.

Rubbing her eyes, Hall said, "You'd better make a start checking what he told us about the sister and the journalist at the paper."

"Do you think he's being straight?"

"Yes. His reaction's genuine enough. Nobody's that good an actor."

"If Belakovsky's as big a deal as he says, what was he doing in a place like this?"

"That's a good question. Who was the fella that sent him the email about Belakovsky being in the country?"

"Jeff Samuels down at Sussex University."

"Get in touch with him and see what he's got to say about it. The whole thing's got a phoney ring to it. We'll have to let the

Russian consulate know what's happened. They'll want to repatriate the body."

"What about Taylor and Emily?"

"Put out an APW. They could be anywhere by now. We can only hope we get lucky. Start with the fight in Haylesbury. Find out the names of the policemen who brought him here and where they're stationed."

"There's going to be a lot of publicity about this—on a national level."

"I know. That's why we're going to do everything by the book."

14

Pritchard stared fixedly at the computer screen. His keen eyes scrutinised the black-and-white video of Emily pushing the wheelchair, in which Taylor was slumped, down the ramp and out of the hospital's fire exit, all the time averting her gaze from the CCTV cameras which overlooked the car park. A real professional, Pritchard thought. This was something that had been planned. Having just killed three people, she was calm and composed, completely aware of her surroundings.

Emily pressed the button on the key fob, and the hazard lights of a black BMW flashed twice. She pushed Taylor up to it and opened the rear door, crouched down and, despite her petite frame, lifted Taylor onto the seat. She slammed the door shut and got in the front. The car shuddered to life and sped off, leaving tyre marks imprinted in the damp tarmac.

The footage came to an abrupt end, and the screen went blank. Pritchard turned away and paced about the room. Anderson sat on the window ledge, watching him through narrowed eyes.

"And that's the clearest footage we've got?" Pritchard said.

"Yes. They haven't updated the cameras since they were installed ten years ago."

"It's worse than useless. It tells us nothing."

"You know that isn't true. From the footage, we know she's a pro."

"True," Pritchard conceded. "But even if she'd looked straight at the camera, all we would've got was a blocky face of pixels and no way to ID her. What about the car?"

"A hire car registered to Belakovsky."

"Belakovsky," Pritchard said, shaking his head. "The circumstances of his death aren't going to be an easy thing to cover up."

"Do you think we should try?"

"Maybe not. Look at the stink the Russians got with Litvinenko. Sometimes it's better to let these things take their natural course."

"You mean, let the police handle it?"

"Wouldn't that be best? If people want to come up with conspiracy theories, they will. They did it with Dr Kelly and the Iraq dossier. Some idiots actually think we murdered him."

"But that's history. Right now, someone was willing to take a big risk in bringing Belakovsky here. I don't think there's any doubt it was Moscow—FSB."

"But who's the girl? Who's she working for?"

"That's the question."

There was a beep from Pritchard's computer, and he went over to it.

"About time," he said. "The police report."

The two men crowded around the screen, reading a transcript of Hall's interview with Peters.

Anderson said, "Did Richmond mention anything about these parents in her report?"

"No. Her mission parameters were to ID Taylor and report back—nothing else."

"You should have given her all the details."

"It doesn't matter. We are where we are."

"What could she want with Taylor?"

"Information. What else!"

"But he knows nothing. He's been missing for three years. He's out of the loop."

"He remembers Stonebridge and Clean Start."

"Only the names. They mean nothing to him."

"Yet, that is. They're probably banking on the fact that amnesia isn't always permanent. With Taylor, they would have detailed information about one of our black ops."

"It's one thing after another at the moment. Let's work with the scenario that the girl's working for the Chinese or Pyongyang. Is she likely to take him out of the country?"

"Pyongyang doesn't have any capabilities. I'm sure it wasn't them. Intelligence is that the Chinese have got several secure locations around the country. We'll keep eyes on them and the motorways, but she's probably ditched the car by now."

The phone on Pritchard's desk rang. He picked it up.

"Yes ... OK ... Call me if you find out anything else."

He hung up.

"Right on cue, the police just found the BMW dumped on a layby in Bristol."

"Bristol?"

"It doesn't mean anything—they could be anywhere in the country by now. This thing was planned. I've got no doubt about that."

"Let's hope they don't make any breakthrough with Taylor. That's all we can do—hope."

There was a strange note in Anderson's voice.

"What do you mean?" Pritchard said.

"There's been speculation for some time that Beijing has perfected the mind sieve."

"We haven't picked anything up on SIGINT."

Pritchard's brows furrowed.

"Who's your source?" he asked.

"MI6 have got an officer deep inside the politburo."

Pritchard bristled; his face puffed with anger.

"Why wasn't I told about this?"

"We wanted to verify its existence first."

"I still should've been told."

"That's something we can discuss at the next JIT."

"You're the one banging on all the time about more cooperation between agencies. And you pull ... never mind. Do we know how it works?"

"Not yet. It could be anything from a machine to a simple pill. But even if they can't get anything useful out of him, they'll use him as a bargaining chip. One way or another, the proverbial shit is going to hit the fan on this one."

15

Pritchard tapped his bony fingers together and stared down at his desk as he spoke to Anne. He was blunt and to the point and could have been dictating a memo to his secretary via his intercom. When he did look up at Anne, who was sitting across from him, hands folded on her lap, it was only briefly to scrutinise her reactions.

Anne said, "There's no doubt in my mind that it was him. I know a man can change in three years, but I'm positive. The eyes, cheeks and forehead—the man I saw was Bruce Taylor."

"What did he say to you? Try to remember his exact words. They may be important."

Anne thought for a moment before recounting the details of her conversation with Taylor.

Stepping away from the door, Anne turned to Taylor and said, "I want to make sure we're alone."

There was such yearning for answers in his eyes that even she—a hardened agent—felt a tug at her heartstrings.

Taylor's mouth moved as if he were about to say something, but he did not.

"You don't remember me?" Anne said.

"No. I'm sorry, but I don't. Were we very close?"

Anne considered and said, "I know Dr Peters wants you to try and remember everything by yourself, but we don't have time for that. I'm your sister."

Taylor's face sagged with relief. For the first time, he felt he was not alone.

"My sister?"

"Yes. Claire."

"How long have I been missing?"

"Three years."

"So long? And you've been looking for me all that time?"

"Of course. It's been hard on everyone."

"My wife?"

"You're not married."

"I hoped I wasn't. I mean, it would be hard to pick up again in a relationship that I have no memory of. What about our parents?"

"They live in London. I haven't had a chance to tell them yet. I wanted to see you before I believed it myself."

"There're so many things I want to know. Have I changed a lot?"

"You've got more grey in your hair, but apart from that, not really."

"And the beard?"

"That's new."

Anne walked up to Taylor, and they embraced. As they parted, Anne ran her hands over Taylor's face and head, smiling self-consciously.

"I want to make sure you're real. It's like a dream. They take good care of you here?"

"Oh, yes. Dr Peters is very interested in my case. I think he's trying to make a name for himself in his field and sees me as an important case study. Not that he doesn't care on a personal level. I know he does."

"I suppose it's your talk of being a spy that's got him so interested?"

"He doesn't ask me that much about it. He doesn't want to encourage any ideas that may not be true. Was I a spy?"

"I don't know. If you were, you didn't tell me. Peters said something about Clean Start and Stonebridge? Do you know what they mean?"

Taylor shook his head.

"No. Do you?"

"No. They're just words to me. So, they mean nothing to you?"

"Nothing. Do you think they're important?"

"What's important is that you're safe."

Pritchard said, "And that's all you asked about Clean Start and Stonebridge?"

"Yes. There didn't seem a lot of point in pressing him. I couldn't have been blunter. He trusted me. I could see it in his eyes. He doesn't remember anything."

"What about Peters? How did he strike you?"

"A bit of a toff. Oxbridge type—confident and a bit full of himself."

"Did he tell you that Belakovsky was coming?"

"No. He seemed excited about something; I just assumed it was because of my meeting with Taylor."

"There was a girl admitted at about the same time you were there. Did you see her?"

"There was a couple with a girl who arrived just as I was leaving—white, middle-aged. There wasn't any family resemblance between either of them and the girl. She looked oriental."

"You would recognise them again?"

"Yes."

Pritchard got up and walked over to a window. He turned back to Anne.

"Taylor and the girl are missing. I'm going to have to send you back into the field again. I know this isn't really a GCHQ thing, but my hand's been forced. We need to find them."

Pritchard went back to his desk, opened a drawer, took out a sheet of paper and handed it to Anne.

"These are the details the parents gave to the hospital. Fictitious, of course, but people sometimes leave subconscious clues. I want you to bring them in."

"Is there any CCTV from the hospital?"

"None of the parents. You're the only person who saw them—apart from Dr Peters. They didn't use the car park so we can assume they arrived by train and then took a taxi. The camera on the gate wasn't working. You're going to have to trawl through the CCTV from the train station. We should get it in an hour."

"What do I do when I find them?"

"Bring them in for questioning. But you're to treat them as hostile. Don't take any chances. I'll authorise you to get a gun from the armoury."

After Anne had departed, Pritchard paced anxiously about the office. He glared at the files on his desk.

"Shit!" he muttered through clenched teeth.

Stepping out of his office into the main open-plan area used by the staff, his eyes met those of Harold Barnes, who was sitting at his desk. Pritchard gave an almost imperceptible nod before going outside.

Anne groaned as she seated herself in front of the monitor. It would be a lot of cups of coffee and a long day sifting the grainy CCTV footage.

However, she was in luck. It only took her thirty minutes before she had reasonable stills of the parents. Standing on the station platform, they looked like an ordinary couple on a day out in the countryside.

The footage from the station car park showed the couple getting into a blue Ford. Anne entered the vehicle registration into the database. Immediately, the names of Ronald and Edith Cartwright flashed up on the screen, accompanied by their address and contact details. As expected, these did not tally with the details given at the hospital.

Even so, Anne got a distinct impression that they were not spooks. They had taken no steps whatsoever to cover their tracks. Indeed, there were many full-face shots on the CCTV video. It could simply have been the case that they had already left the country, and hence there was no need to take any precautions. Whatever the reason, she still had to go to the address to find out one way or the other.

16

The corridor was cold, ascetic. Taylor stood, staring at the rows of closed steel doors extending on both sides of him, not knowing how he had got here or where *here* even was.

The polished hard-stone floor gleamed dully under a strip light. Taylor glanced around, confused and feeling very alone. His thick breath hung in the frigid air, goose bumps rising on his arms.

All was quiet, not a sound to be heard, except his heavy breathing. He walked up to the nearest door, his heels tapping emptily against the floor. From behind the door, the sudden clatter of something metallic falling to the floor broke the silence and sent his heart pounding against his chest. He took a tentative step back and froze, listening intently.

Footsteps could be heard approaching from the other side, and the door handle began to rattle violently. He waited for the door to swing open. But it did not, and the rattling abruptly ceased.

For a whole minute, he stood, frozen, holding his breath.

"Is anyone there?" he said, managing to keep his voice level.

No response.

He looked around. If he were to find out where he was, he would have to open one of the doors. He grabbed the ice-cold handle and slowly pushed down on it, his body tense, braced for whatever or whoever may be on the other side. The door fell back, and a rush of cold, fetid air hit him in the face. The room was in black velvet darkness and icily cold, the distant whirr of a fan the only sound to be heard. He fumbled in the darkness until he found the light switch and turned it on. A fitful light illuminated the room. His blood ran cold.

Seven bodies, partially covered by white sheets, exposed from the chest up, were laid out on steel autopsy slabs. Tied to their big toes were paper name tags. Taylor walked tentatively up to the nearest body. The face of the cadaver was hard and marble white, livid blue veins protruding in its temples. He was a young man, no older than twenty-five. Between his eyes, a black entry wound of a .22 calibre bullet encrusted with black blood.

"I know you," Taylor whispered.

He reached over and checked the name tag—scrawled on it, in black marker, a single word: murderer.

He looked across at the next body. This one had several bullet holes in the torso. A middle-aged man who had once been big and athletic but turned to fat, his face contorted in a mottled, ugly grimace of pain.

Taylor frantically rushed between the bodies. All of them had multiple gunshot wounds, and all had murderer writ large on their name tags. However, what disturbed him the most was that all the faces were familiar. Somewhere, he had seen them before.

When he reached the final body, he said, "What does this mean?"

He froze as he sensed a presence. Slowly, he turned around. A man was sitting on the floor in the far corner, legs crossed, staring at the floor, sobbing.

"Hello," Taylor said.

The man, absorbed in his grief, made no response.

Taylor walked up to him.

"*Warum? Warum?*" the man blabbered.

Taylor's shadow fell over him, and the man slowly raised his head.

"You!" Taylor gasped. "It's you!"

The man whom he had dreamt about so often since his admission to the hospital got unsteadily to his feet. For a long time, the two men stared at each other. The man's eyes were filled with tears, and Taylor could feel his cold breath on his face.

The man reached down and unzipped his hoodie to reveal a plain black T-shirt. Beneath it, something moved, the cloth rippling as it did so.

Taylor's stomach was in knots, his face breaking out in a cold sweat.

The man yelled, "*Bitte töte mich nicht. Ich habe eine Frau und Sohn!*"

In a sudden violent outburst, he tore off his T-shirt to reveal his bare chest. Beneath the skin, something was moving, the skin rising and falling as it moved within the chest cavity.

Taylor took deep gulps.

The man screamed as the grotesque, blood-drenched head of a woman burst out of his chest. Blood sprayed onto Taylor's face. The man's body crumpled and fell to the floor like a dried-up husk. Out stepped a woman, drenched in blood, her hair clinging to her face, a newborn baby cradled in her arms.

17

Taylor awoke with a start, gasping for breath. His eyes flashed open; his mind was immediately alert and hyperaware of his surroundings. He was lying in bed. A light shone from under the door in the corner of the room. He lay still, his eyes darting around the room, which was in a disordered state.

Books with pages covered in handwritten annotations lay open on a desk. There was a big armchair by the bed, in front of it, a low coffee table. Beside the door was a bookcase crammed full of almanacks, encyclopaedias and thick, dusty reference books.

From the other side of the door, he could hear the clatter of dishes and running water. He got up, feeling weak and lethargic, walked slowly over to the window and drew apart the curtains. The gold of the sunset burned, the trees that lined the residential street casting long shadows over the parked cars.

He spun around as the door opened, and Emily entered. She was holding a tray on which was a steaming bowl of soup and a bread roll. Startled, she took a step back.

Nervously smiling, she said, "You're awake. I made you some soup."

She placed the tray on the coffee table. Taylor said nothing but watched her closely.

Finally, he said, "Where am I?"

"Have some of the soup first," Emily said. "It's been a long time since you've eaten."

Taylor stared at her, rapidly breathing, eyes fixed on the half-open door.

"I'll tell you everything, but eat something first," Emily said.

Taylor continued to stare at the door.

"You're safe here," Emily said,

She walked over to him and tenderly touched his arm.

"OK," Taylor said levelly.

He sat down on the armchair; Emily seated herself on the edge of the bed.

She said, "This place belongs to a friend of mine—Professor Cooper. He's gone to an academic conference in Manchester. We don't have to worry about being disturbed."

Taylor spooned some of the hot soup into his mouth. It immediately worked on his stomach but tasted strange. He put down the spoon.

"I've had some. Now tell me what happened. How did I get out of the hospital?"

"You don't remember?"

"No."

"What's the last thing you do remember?"

Taylor took a moment before answering, "I was in bed, and a nurse gave me some pills for my scan."

"They drugged you—probably with a benzodiazepine—and tried to lobotomise you. That's why you don't remember anything. It causes paralysis and short-term memory loss. Have some more soup."

"It tastes wrong."

"That'll be the effect of the benzodiazepine."

"Who are *they*?"

"FSB."

Taylor stared at her, waiting expectantly.

"The Russian secret service."

"You mean, Belakovsky was a spy?"

"A sleeper. I had my suspicions when he arrived; it didn't make any sense that he would come to a small hospital like that for what was a routine case."

"Who are you—*really*?"

Tears stood in Emily's eyes.

With intense feeling, she said, "You still don't remember me?"

Taylor said nothing.

"We used to work together. You were my contact here in London."

"Then, I am a spy?"

"Yes," Emily said, nodding. "And more."

Taylor got to his feet.

"Yes?" he said, his voice taut with expectation.

Emily got up and walked over to him. She looked up into his eyes, and they kissed. She drew her head back and buried it in his chest, her arms wrapped around him.

"I always knew you'd made it out," she said. "They said you were dead, but I never believed them. Never!"

Taylor held her tight. His feelings towards her had not simply been those of a frightened, lonely man seeking friendship—they ran much deeper. There had always existed between them a connection that no amnesia could fully erase.

He held her head in his hands, tilted it upwards and kissed her.

"I want to know everything," he said.

Wiping away tears, Emily said, "I don't know *everything*."

"But you know who I am?"

"We never spoke about our pasts. It was easier that way."

The two of them sat down on the edge of the bed, Taylor holding Emily's hand.

She said, "I was recruited by MI6 when I was in my final year at Tsinghua University, where I studied political science. I'd always been careful in all my dissertations never to reveal that I have a western, democratic view of the world. Still, one of my lecturers—who MI6 had already recruited—suspected I did. He knew I was never destined to be just another party stooge.

"He took a big risk in revealing himself. He told me that there was an opportunity for me to work for MI6 but that I should go home and think it over before deciding. I didn't need to think it over; it was so exciting to be able to make a difference.

"Of course, it was dangerous. If I were ever exposed, it would be certain death. Even with the censorship in the country, I was well aware of the injustices that happened every day, people murdered, disappeared or sent off for re-education.

"I had to be careful and trust no one; it's routine for the government to even recruit children as spies and informants. Our culture is one based on blind devotion to the motherland.

"They started me off small. My first job was to collect envelopes from various drop boxes and then drop them off at other locations. What happened to them after that, I don't know. It may all have been just a way of testing my trustworthiness.

"After I graduated, I got a job in the Ministry of Foreign Affairs. I'm pretty sure MI6 had someone working on the inside to get me that job. It allowed me to travel abroad without arousing suspicion. My first trip was to London. While I was there, I was transferred to MI5."

"And that's where we met?"

"Yes."

"And I never told you what I did?"

"No, and I never asked. It wouldn't have made any difference if you'd been an admin clerk or a field agent. For security reasons, we weren't able to talk about our work. None of it mattered to me. I was in love with you."

Taylor got up.

"I've had dreams. I had one just now. I was in a morgue; dead bodies were laid out on slabs. They all had name tags with murderer written on them."

Emily got to her feet and said, "It's just a dream. Dreams aren't memories."

"No. I remember their faces. I've seen them before, and there's one face that keeps coming up in *all* my dreams. He spoke to me. He said ..."

Taylor sat down and screwed up his face as he tried to remember what the man had said.

"What did he say?" Emily asked.

"He spoke in German. I can see his face, as clear as yours, but I don't remember what he said."

"It doesn't mean you're a murderer."

"I didn't just drop off envelopes either. And what about the fight in the high street. I almost killed a man with my bare hands. Where did I learn to do that? When did I go missing?"

"Three years ago. You were working on the Stonebridge case—you told me that much. You left on a Friday morning, and that was the last time I saw you."

Emily wiped away tears from her cheeks.

"Why didn't you tell me all this at the hospital? Why all this secrecy?"

"I didn't know if we were being watched."

"Peters?"

"Yes. Or one of the nurses."

"Are you going to bring me in?"

"No. It's not going to be that easy. Belakovsky knew you were at the hospital because someone tipped him off."

"FSB."

"No, someone from our side. The agency isn't clean. Bringing you in could be just what they're counting on."

"You're not working directly for MI5?"

"No. I'm playing a lone hand. I've got a few friends helping me. They're the ones who found out that you'd been admitted to the hospital. I can't be sure you'll be safe if you go back in."

"You think they'll try to kill me again?"

"If you were important enough to risk Belakovsky—yes."

"And Belakovsky?"

"Dead. He killed himself."

Taylor fell back in his chair.

"So, what do we do?"

"First, we need to let the benzodiazepine pass through your system."

"And then?"

"We need to find out exactly what Clean Start is. Then we'll have an idea about who's trying to eliminate you, one of ours or FSB."

"And if I can't remember anything … elimination."

Taylor was developing a deep dislike of the bland, yet vicious, argot of these agencies, which operated in the shadows of society.

"There are ways to make you remember," Emily said.

Her tone was strange.

She got up and walked over to a stained bureau, pulled open a drawer and took out a small black plastic case. She pushed down on two latches, opened the case and took out a little black box.

"We've been working on experimental equipment and drugs at the agency to help people better recall things they forget due to stress. The results have been good on test subjects."

"How does it work?"

"I'm not sure about the technical side. You take a pill. It relaxes you, and you go into what's called an alpha state where you're receptive to suggestions. It's a kind of hypnosis."

"Is it safe?"

"It's still undergoing trials. We've been working on it for a couple of years and haven't had any problems with it—as far as side effects."

"Whether it's safe or not, I have to try," Taylor said. "It's my only chance to find out who I am."

18

It was an ordinary residential street: bay fronted, semi-detached houses with small compact lawns. Anne got out of her car and walked up to the front gate of number twenty-seven. As with all the houses on the street, it had a shared drive that led directly to a rear garden. Parked in the drive was the Cartwrights' blue Ford.

Even though it was midday, all the curtains in the house were drawn. Stuffed in the letterbox were leaflets and junk mail. Anne rang the bell, heard several chimes from inside but got no response. She forced the post through the letterbox, and it fell to the floor with a thud. Crouching down on her haunches, she pushed back the letterbox's flap and peered inside. To her alarm, there were hundreds of letters, leaflets and newspapers on the floor—more than a family would reasonably expect to receive in years. Putting her ear to the open letterbox, she listened and could just make out the distant sound of a running tap.

A cat meandered up the footpath and started purring as it rubbed its head against her leg. Anne, who adored cats, knelt down to stroke it. Immediately, she froze, an ominous chill of fear settling over her. She ran her hand over its fur, which was covered in red blotches and checked for any injury. There was none. It was not the cat's blood. She got up and glanced around at the row of parked cars that lined the road. They were all unoccupied, and there was no one on the street. A white Transit van turned into the road. Anne reached inside her jacket for her gun. The van slowed as it approached, and the driver peered at her with mild curiosity before speeding off.

Anne let out a breath and withdrew her shaking hand from her jacket, and took a moment to compose herself. It had been a long time since she had been touched by fear, and she began to doubt if she still had it in her to master her emotions. A year sitting behind a desk had made her soft.

She stepped over the low brick wall which separated the front garden from the drive and slowly made her way to the rear garden. The drive had not been well maintained, weeds poking through the cracked cement. When she reached the end of the drive, she stopped. The back garden spread out before her. The Cartwrights were a couple who took pride in their garden.

On seeing her, a blackbird that had been gorging itself on the ripe yellow berries of a pyracantha bush flew away, its fluttering form disappearing into the distance. The garden was lined with various evergreen shrubs, the border separated, with ceramic edgings, from an immaculately mowed rectangular lawn. In the far corner, in the dappled shade of a hawthorn tree, she could just make out the black outline of a body.

Taking her gun from her jacket, she sprinted across the lawn, blood rushing in her ears. She reached the tree and immediately recognised the prostrate body as that of the man who had called himself Emily's father. He was lying on his back, an empty plastic bird feeder clasped in his cold, white fingers. There was a single bullet wound in his forehead. His body was rigid; he had been dead some time. A beetle crawled out of his nose. Anne turned away, nausea rising in her.

Raising her hand to shield her eyes from the sun, she looked up at the house. Unlike the front windows, the rear curtains were not drawn. Even so, she could not see into the dark rooms.

It was now that she noticed that the back door was ajar, rocking on its hinges. She sprinted over to it, threw it open, and rushed into the kitchen. It was a small room with a fridge, cooker and work surface. The tap was running, the sink full of water, dirty plates and a plastic cup bobbing up and down. She stepped into the adjoining dining room. A table was laid out, a bowl of beige paste which had once been cereal, beside it, a rack of stale toast and a half-drunk mug of coffee. For over a minute, she held her breath and listened but heard nothing.

She went into the hallway. Slumped in the corner was a postman, a small black hole bored into his forehead. His eyes were rolled over, yellow with death. His red bag, half full of letters, had tipped over and spilt its contents across the floor.

She looked up the short flight of carpeted stairs. Her gun held tight in her hand, she went up, pausing after each step to listen. She reached the landing and stopped. Two legs protruded from the half-open bathroom door. She tentatively pushed back the door to reveal a middle-aged woman lying face down on the tiled floor, her frayed black hair matted in the red pulp which had once been the back of her head.

What was impressive about the killings was that there had been no stray bullets. One shot had been all the assassin had needed to dispatch each target. Anne pictured the scene. The assassin had walked from the street into the rear garden and shot the man. The back door open, he had gone in and shot the woman in the back of the head as she readied herself for the day. The job done; he must have left at the same time that the postman arrived. The assassin had lured him in and killed him with his signature headshot. The headshots showed confidence. It would have been safer to shoot at the body first and finish off to the head if needed.

Anne went into the bedroom and sat down on the bed. The Cartwrights may not have had many friends, so they might not be missed, even for a few days. But the postman who was young and wore a wedding band would surely be missed soon.

She got up and began searching through the nightstand's drawers. Her attention was drawn to a small card under a jar of moisturiser. With the tips of her fingers, she carefully lifted the jar and picked up the card. It was the business card of Edward Woodstein, talent agent.

19

Taylor opened his eyes and squinted. His vision was blurry, and he could only make out vague shapes around the bright desk lamp that was pointed at his face. He reached out and pushed it away as Emily's black figure came over and turned it off.

His vision gradually became clearer, and he looked up at the clock on the wall. An hour had elapsed since Emily had set up the black box. As it powered up, LEDs flickered, and a control panel of three touch-sensitive buttons illuminated. Housed within its flimsy case were circuit boards and a microprocessor with the potential to bring back the man he had been. Taylor's stomach had knotted with anticipation when Emily had started to attach leads to it. She had taken meticulous care applying the gel and attaching the sensors to his arms and temples. Soon, a dozen wires were attached to his body, each leading back to the little black box.

Emily pressed a button, and several LEDs began to flash. A tingling sensation spread across his temples and arms. She handed him a red pill. For an instant, their eyes met. He swallowed it and quickly became drowsy, his eyelids growing heavy. Emily, sitting across from him, her pen hovering expectantly over a fresh page on her notepad, was the last thing he remembered.

Now an hour had passed, and Taylor remembered nothing of it. No new memories lingered. Had it worked? An hour of his life had elapsed, never to be lived again.

In silence, Emily removed the last sensor attached to his temple. She did not say a word and was in a sombre mood.

Taylor rubbed his temple.

"How do you feel?" Emily asked.

"A bit drowsy."

"It takes a few hours to wear off."

Emily started wrapping the cables around her hand and tied them together with a plastic ribbon, carefully putting them back in the case.

"Did it work?"

"Yes."

Emily picked up the black box and put it back in its case.

"What did I say?"

"You're sure you want me to tell you?" Emily asked, an ominous note in her voice.

"Yes."

Emily closed the case, the catch fastening with a click, and took her notepad from the table.

"You're thirty-two years old. You're not married and have no children. After graduating from UCL, you were recruited by MI5. You worked as an officer for A Branch. You ran their network in Berlin. Your primary purpose was to recruit new agents. You worked with Glover, Franks and Gillette."

Taylor shook his head; the names meant nothing to him.

"Go on."

"You ran the network for four years. In that time, you turned two Russian agents. But when Glover and Franks were found dead within days of each other, the network was disbanded. You helped the two doubles and Gillette get to London via Amsterdam.

"Although two of your agents were dead, the network was deemed a success. You were then recruited to be part of a joint MI5, GCHQ programme called Clean Start."

Emily turned the page.

"Clean Start was a programme designed to infiltrate Chinese sleeper cells based here in the UK. You were put in charge of a network based in London. Your team successfully uncovered over ten cells in the first year alone. But it got harder as they started to recognise your team's surveillance and infiltration techniques.

"So, your cell turned its attention to Russian agents. That was when you went to Stonebridge. I couldn't penetrate any memories after that. Whatever happened is buried too deep in your mind. That or your mind has put up some sort of defence mechanism."

Emily gave Taylor a moment to take in what she had said.

"At least we know what Clean Start is," he said.

"It explains why the Russians are so desperate to get their hands on you. They've been having problems with infiltration for years. You're the key to their getting a grip on it."

"And my sister?"

"You don't have a sister. She might be part of some parallel op they're running."

"Or there could be a third party involved. There's no shortage of people who want a piece of me."

Taylor got up and added, "At the moment, it's all just facts. I don't have any emotional connection to any of it."

"You will, in time."

"Will I? Will I ever remember these things as my memories, or will they always be like things I've read in a book? Memories are personal. These aren't."

"Do you want to come in?"

"Yes, I think it's for the best. The only people who can help me now are in GCHQ and MI5. They know who I am. Can you make contact?"

"Yes. The Emergency Line. I can't call from here because they'll trace it."

"Why should that matter? We're on the same side. I'm one of *their* officers."

"It's a dangerous thing to trust people. To them, you're an asset. Don't think they won't throw you to the wolves if they see any benefit in it. Utility is their prime motive."

The statement shook Taylor. Had he too been as cold as these faceless spymasters of which Emily was painting a picture? He had worked for them for years. You didn't do a job like that without taking on their values.

Emily added, "A lot of them are relics from the Cold War era. They think in terms of dogma and ideology. But allegiances, like uniforms, can be quickly changed. The life of one person doesn't mean anything to them when it's stacked up against the war as a whole. Everyone's expendable."

"You haven't told me everything."

Emily made no response.

"The bodies in my dreams. I've killed people, haven't I?"

"Yes."

Taylor slumped down in the chair.

"That was a different person," Emily said. "It wasn't you."

"The dreams aren't just dreams."

"No."

Taylor thrust his face into his hands. It felt to him as if nothing good had survived—only a feeling of remorseless guilt.

20

Surveying the circular garden at the centre of the Doughnut, Barnes said, "They haven't used this space to anything near its potential. I thought they were going to do so much more with it."

Pritchard turned around on the bench where he was sitting and watched Barnes bend down and pick up a stray twig on the damp path.

"It looks OK to me," Pritchard said.

"To *you*. It's just grass. They haven't even taken good care of it. When was the last time it was mowed? Weeds are growing over there. There's so much more they could have done. If I had a free hand, I'd build a Japanese water garden over there and plant lilac bushes and azaleas in front of that wall."

Barnes smiled, threw away the twig and added, "You really should try to take more of an interest in things other than your work. It would give you more to talk about with Melissa. Marriage is something you have to work at."

"You're always so concerned with her," Pritchard said. "Why? Are you fucking her?"

"That's crude, Lewis. But would you really care if I made a cuckold out of you?"

Pritchard scowled and said, "You know the arrangement I have with her."

"Of course. It's a pity you can't appreciate her. But to answer your question. No, I'm not fucking her."

Pritchard shot Barnes a hard glance. The confident, self-assured Barnes repelled him. His tweed jacket, Oxford shirt with buttoned-down collars and his cashmere pullover were so clichéd. How had someone so superficial ever got to the position of deputy of K Division? Pritchard thought. But he knew the answer, and it irritated him.

Barnes said, "I heard she turned a lot of heads at Black's leaving bash last night."

"She was OK."

"Come now. She was spectacular. By the way, she told me what happened. If you start treating her that way, things can quickly unravel."

Pritchard's face reddened.

"She hates me, and I don't blame her."

"Calm down, old chap. I know we're alone out here, but you don't want to take any chances of being overheard."

Pritchard took a deep breath and glanced up at the myriad of windows that surrounded them.

He said, "Enough of Melissa. I didn't come here to talk about her. I've got more pressing matters on my mind."

"Taylor?"

"Yes, Taylor! There was someone outside my house last night, watching. Do you know anything about it?"

Barnes shook his head and took a packet of cigarettes from his pocket, proffering them to Pritchard.

With a dismissive wave of his hand, Pritchard said, "Just answer the question."

Barnes shrugged and said, "No. It's the first I've heard about it."

"Don't bullshit me!"

Barnes took out a cigarette, tapped it on the packet, and considered Pritchard as if he were an unruly child. His patronising expression annoyed Pritchard no end.

"I'm not bullshitting you. If I had sent someone to keep tabs on you, I wouldn't have had them sit outside your house. Whoever was watching you wanted you to know that you were under surveillance. Do you think Lyle's got something to do with it?"

"I've got my suspicions."

"You don't look well. Why don't you take some time off?"

"At a time like this?"

Blowing out a cloud of smoke, Barnes said, "Leave it to me. I'll keep you up to date. It might be better if you kept a low profile."

"What are you getting at?"

"Nothing. I'm just trying to help. This should be a team effort. Share the load."

Pritchard said nothing.

"Why do you suspect Lyle?" Barnes asked.

"He was talking with Charters at the party before I got there."

Barnes smiled and said, "A conspiracy? I do so like them."

"Scoff if you like, but there's something to it."

"So, he was talking to Charters. That's only to be expected: they're old friends, and we're all part of the JIT fold."

"They stopped talking when I joined them. There wasn't any reason for Lyle to be there. It was a GCHQ affair."

"He's a friend of Jason Black. If you took more of an interest in the personal lives of people—"

"No, they're up to something."

"I think you're being a touch paranoid. Is that all you're going on—a bit of chit-chat you were excluded from?"

"He said things."

"What things?"

"It doesn't matter."

"Did you bring up Taylor with Charters?"

"Yes."

"Come on, Lewis. Do I have to prod all your responses from you?"

"He didn't want to talk about him—bad form to talk shop. He was very calm about the whole thing, just like Lyle."

"You'd feel better if they were panicking? They're experienced men. They've seen this kind of thing before. Charters goes back to that Geoffrey Prime business."

"So do I, and I can tell you that no one was calm then. They were all running around like headless chickens, trying to find the leak. Maggie took a dump on us for that when she sanctioned all those reports and committees."

"You think he's keeping you out of the loop."

"It looks that way."

"Let us consider what we do know."

"It's a sure thing the girl's working for the Chinese."

"We haven't picked up anything. All we're getting is static. They've put a lid on things."

"That means they're going to try and get them out of the country."

"Did you get that from our source?"

"No. It's just a gut feeling. It's what I would do."

"Then we wait. The police have put out an APW. But I still don't see why you're getting so concerned. What's the worst thing that can happen?"

"Anderson thinks the mind sieve's for real. They could make Taylor remember."

"Remember what? We both know he's not Taylor. Whoever they've got, they won't learn anything from him."

"You're too sure of yourself. There's a lot more to this. Whoever the man is, he was put in that hospital by someone to provoke a reaction. And he got one."

Barnes finished off his cigarette and looked around for a bin.

He said, "I suppose you've sent Anne Richmond after the old couple?"

"She's making enquiries."

Barnes shook his head and said, "Hunting down spies isn't really our thing. You know, if you're worried about Lyle, you could bug his office. It wouldn't be a difficult thing to do."

Pritchard shook his head and said, "No. it's too risky."

"Then sit back and relax. There's no point in getting worked up about the whole business. Things will work out. They always do."

21

Edward Woodstein's office was on the second floor of a squat two-storey building in an industrial park. Across from his office was a gym. He stood at the window, smoking a cigarette, watching a young woman, sweat gleaming on her arms and neck, as she pulled the levers of a cross-trainer. A couple of male bodybuilders were lifting weights whilst another posed in front of a mirror. A friend joined him, and they compared biceps. What a narcissistic lot, Woodstein thought.

Adjacent to the gym was a car park, which was empty, except for Woodstein's ten-year-old Toyota. Black, shrivelled up buddleias sprouted up from beneath the industrial park's rusty metal perimeter fence.

This was not the lifestyle he had imagined when, five years ago, he had started his agency in what he imagined to be the glitzy world of entertainment. He exhaled a cloud of smoke, watching with interest as a black Mercedes pulled up in the car park. He was even more interested when a woman—an attractive woman—got out. He hoped she represented a major production company.

After all these years, he had depressingly few connections in the business. However, he was the eternal optimist. People underestimated the role luck played in life. Hard work was important, but you still needed luck, and he felt he was due a truckload.

The woman's car and sharp trouser suit connoted money and success. Whenever Woodstein met a potential client, he always tried to give the impression that his books were full and that he was very selective about whom he took on. But the truth was he represented a handful of mediocre Z-list clients for whom he could barely secure a living, let alone himself. Most of them were suited to niche jobs; they had unusual talents but nothing mainstream.

He took a long drag on his cigarette and went over to his desk, straightened up some papers before stubbing out his cigarette on a half-eaten roll which he threw in the wastepaper basket. He opened a window, letting in a cold breeze that immediately freshened up the small office. He sat down and picked up the phone and, with his free hand, began to doodle on a scrap of paper. The woman's dark outline appeared behind the frosted glass door panel emblazoned with Edward Woodstein – Talent Agency. He sighed. He should have had it cleaned; it was covered in dust.

Into the phone, he bellowed, "No way, not a chance! I can't do it for less than twenty thousand. Yeah, I know what you said."

He stopped when Anne tapped on the door.

"Come in, come in."

Anne entered. He waved at her, indicating that she should take a seat in a grubby chair with blue leather upholstery. Woodstein nodded in response to her look of enquiry, and she seated herself.

"I can't go any lower than twenty. That's what you're going to have to pay. It's a free market. If you want to get another girl … OK … OK … Listen, when you've had a chance to check with Gordon, let me know. I only talk in hard numbers."

Woodstein hung up.

"That was John Blake. He's casting for a new film. These Hollywood bigwigs always like to play hardball. How can I help you, Miss …?"

"Anne Richmond. You're Edward Woodstein?"

"You can call me Ned. All my friends do. I helped a lot of big stars take their first steps in the business."

Anne looked dubiously around.

"This office is only temporary. My London one's being refurbished, and there was a mix up with the letting agent. Are you in the business?"

"I'm interested in a middle-aged couple, Ronald and Edith Cartwright, who did some work for you yesterday at Mountview hospital."

Woodstein's eyes narrowed.

"Yes. How do you know about them?"

Anne took a small card from her pocket and handed it to him. He slowly read the card and flashed a glance up at her. The photograph on the police ID was her. He swallowed and handed it back.

"They're not in any trouble, are they?"

"No."

"You don't mind if I smoke?"

"Go ahead."

Woodstein opened a drawer and took out a packet of cigarettes and a lighter. Hands shaking, he drew out a cigarette and lit it.

"I've never had anything to do with the police before."

"Tell me about the Cartwrights."

"Oh, yeah, the Cartwrights. Nice couple. I took them on about five months ago. They've mostly been doing work as extras. It didn't pay much, but they didn't care. It was more of a hobby for them."

"Who arranged the job?"

"I got a call from the manager of a small production company in Essex. He explained the job—some kind of reality TV show—and what kind of people he was looking for. The Cartwrights fitted the bill."

"Did you meet him?"

"No. Everything was done over the phone."

"I see. So, you never met him face to face."

"No."

"And payment?"

Woodstein considered, rapidly smoking.

Anne said, "I'm not from HMRC. Your tax affairs aren't of any interest to me."

She didn't want to risk Woodstein becoming defensive and opted for the direct approach.

"The Cartwrights are dead."

Woodstein's face blanched.

"What!" he exclaimed, his hand involuntarily coming up and covering his mouth.

"They were murdered yesterday."

"And you think I had something to do with it?"

"No. I know you didn't. The job was a setup. I need to know the facts of what happened. How were you paid?"

"C-cash. After we agreed on the fee, a courier arrived with the money."

"Is that normal?"

"No. I'll be straight with you. Things are tight. I need all the work I can get. If I'd known this would happen … But how could I … I …"

"How much were you paid?"

"Five thousand."

"Is that the going rate for a job like this?"

"No, the usual rate's five hundred a day, but they sounded desperate, so I took a chance and upped the price. He didn't haggle—agreed right off the bat."

"Did anything strike you about him? Did he have an accent? Was there anything unusual about the way he spoke?"

"I'm pretty sure he was foreign. His English was too exact—too grammatically correct—as if he'd learnt it from a textbook."

The smooth purr of a car pulling up outside drew their attention. Anne got up and went over to the window. Woodstein joined her at her side. A black Mercedes had pulled up and parked next to Anne's car. A slim man with slicked back, jet-black hair, wearing shades, got out. He looked across at Anne's car and then up at the office. Anne took Woodstein by the arm and stepped back from the window.

Whether she could somehow see the almost imperceptible bulge of the concealed gun beneath his jacket or whether there was something about the cold, calm expression on his face, Anne had acquired a sixth sense from years of working in the field and knew the man's deadly purpose in being here.

Woodstein said, "W-what is it?"

"We have to get out."

"W-Why?"

"He's here to kill you."

The phone on the desk rang.

Anne said, "Don't answer it."

"What are you talking about?" Woodstein said, reaching over to pick it up.

"You answer that, and we're both dead."

Woodstein's body was beginning to shake convulsively. Anne grabbed him by the shoulders.

"Get a grip," she said.

"T-This isn't h-happening. Tell me it's a j-joke. Tell S-Stevens he got me. It was S-Stevens who s-sent you?"

Anne slapped Woodstein hard across the face and drew her Glock-17 from her jacket. It had a sobering effect on Woodstein.

"This is no joke," she said.

Woodstein gulped and turned to the door as he heard soft footsteps ascending the stairs.

Anne said, "Don't make a sound and do exactly what I say."

Woodstein nodded.

Anne waved her gun at the door and said, "Stand over there."

Woodstein took up position beside the door. Anne crouched behind the desk, and with bated breath, waited. Woodstein clenched tight his eyes. Anne clasped the grip of her gun and slipped her finger over the trigger. Beads of sweat were trickling down Woodstein's face, his clammy hands trembling. He pressed his back tight against the wall and, for an instant, managed to pry open his eyes and look over at Anne.

Her face remained inscrutable, and her eyes fixed on the door. For over a minute, no one moved. There was complete silence, no shadow in the door's frosted pane. Anne peered down to look through the crack under the door. Nothing but the dim light from the corridor.

She turned back to Woodstein. A shadow flitted across the frosted glass and was gone before she had time to react. A spasm of uncontrollable fear flashed across Woodstein's face. Anne knew that he was going to run. His nerve would not hold. Tensely, she licked her dry lips. Don't do it! Don't move, her mind screamed. He was at the limit of his self-control.

Again, the phone on the desk rang. After several rings, it stopped and a period of silence ensued. It was no more than thirty seconds but felt like an age to Anne.

She looked across at Woodstein. His eyes were now as big as saucers. Suddenly, he began to blabber and cry. Tearing himself away from the wall, he ran for cover behind his desk.

"No!" Anne screamed.

A shadow sprang up from behind the door, and a deafening crack cut through the air. The door's pane shattered, and glass rained down onto the floor and desk. Books, papers and filing drawers on Woodstein's desk flew in all directions as the thud, thud, thud of gunfire ensued. Anne rolled onto her side and returned a quick burst of fire. The wooden door split apart; the central panel riddled with bullet holes.

Woodstein had collapsed into a heap on the floor. All fell silent. The smell of cordite hung heavy in the air. Anne got to her feet and ran over to Woodstein. He was dead; a bullet had passed straight through the back of his head.

She heard footsteps receding down the stairs and made her way to the window and watched as the assassin leapt into his car. There was a trail of blood on the ground. Tyres screeched as he sped out of the car park and drove off.

Anne got out her phone.

"Anne Richmond. Code: Red. Black Mercedes. Registration: L1729 SRA, headed westbound to the A312 junction 12."

"Are there any casualties?" the operator asked.

Anne looked down at Woodstein's body.

22

"You're very quiet tonight, dear," Margaret said as she strolled into the living room. She was in a relaxed mood, wearing beige slacks, slippers and a mauve cotton blouse, her blonde hair spilling over her shoulders.

Sitting in his armchair, Anderson gloomily stared ahead, watching the flames lick the wooden logs in the fireplace. He had assured Charters that he would be able to keep a lid on matters, but the whole thing had blown up in his face, and he had a dark foreboding that things would only get worse.

"Dear?"

Anderson looked up at Margaret, who smiled sympathetically, handing him his mug of tea before taking a seat on the sofa beside him.

Absently putting the mug down on the table, Anderson said, "There's a lot going on at the moment."

"I don't suppose it's anything you can talk about?"

Anderson reached over and clasped Margaret's hand. They had been married for nearly twenty-five years. She was the one constant in his life, the one person he could always rely upon to take his side.

"No, I'm afraid not."

Margaret looked at him with understanding eyes.

"I've never seen you like this. I'm always here for you. You know that."

"I know, dear. I know," Anderson said, patting her hand.

He regretted his decision to accede to Pritchard's view that it was better to act with caution. He should have stood by his own instincts and got Taylor out of the hospital.

After all, he was the one with years of experience in making difficult decisions in the field. Pritchard was just a code breaker, a paper pusher who knew nothing of field ops. And yet, he had given in to him. What grated most in Anderson's mind was that deep down, he knew he had always been the victim of an inferiority complex and that had been the reason he had not stood his ground.

He was a big bear of a man who had always had to contend with the stereotype that big meant clumsy and slow. In the world of counterintelligence, ops never ran smoothly. It was never seen as a slur on his ability when things didn't go to plan. Real-world ops were complex, and one could never plan for all eventualities. Even so, one setback was all it took for the impression of his clumsiness to be confirmed in his mind.

He had ascended quickly through the ranks of the organisation. There was always that doubt that he had not earned his position but had been given an unfair advantage, over the likes of Pritchard, with favours from friends he had made during his time at Oxford. He knew of Pritchard's background spent living in poverty and somewhat envied him. Pritchard had earned his place—no doubt about it. Anderson was not prone to bouts of self-pity, and he knew it would have been perverse to wish his upbringing had been harsher. How many people would have envied him his comfortable start in life?

Lost in thought, he said, "I guess I should stand up for myself."

"What do you mean?"

Breaking from his introspections, Anderson stared at Margaret.

"I … I was just thinking."

"I know exactly what you were thinking. You've earned everything in life. Don't fall into that old trap of thinking that you wouldn't have succeeded if it hadn't been for your upbringing. You should never be apologetic for what you are."

"I know. You're right," Anderson said, lacking conviction.

"Every day, you have to make hundreds of critical decisions. No one expects you to be perfect. If you make a wrong decision, don't dwell on it."

The hallway phone rang, and Margaret left to answer it.

It was always in the evening that Anderson's inner demon of inferiority reared its ugly head. He walked over to the window and looked up at the new moon hanging high in the sky. Maybe we're more susceptible to our fears at night, he mused. Perhaps there was some primaeval force that brought them to the surface.

He went over to the shelf crammed full of CDs and selected one, putting it into the player. There was a momentary hum from the speakers, and then the sweet, melodic sounds of Mozart's *Eine Kleine Nachtmusik* filled the room. He pressed a button, and it skipped forward to the *Romanze*—his favourite part. Closing his eyes, he let out a deep breath. Working alone, not trusting anyone, was bound to expose latent neurosis.

His thoughts turned to his old friend, Colonel Paris, who he had not seen for many years. How much simpler life would have been if he had followed a career in the military? These spy games were not something he enjoyed. In the army, he would be dealing with straightforward, straight-talking people. There was a clear and obvious enemy on the battlefield. In contrast, counterintelligence was a war without end, a war in which today's enemies were tomorrow's friends. Ever since primitive man, no more than intelligent apes, had formed cliques, they had spied on one another for no other reason than that they could. It was a tendency seemingly hardwired into the human psyche.

He wished he had never heard of Clean Start, but since it was a black op set up to assassinate domestic and overseas targets, it made sense that it should be run under the auspices of both MI5 and MI6. Charters had been the one who had come up with the idea, and so, GCHQ was also included in it. They all had joint responsibility for it. But now, each of the agencies couldn't get far enough away from it.

He had not been directly involved in the Stonebridge investigation. It occurred to him that most of what he knew about it was from what people had told him, things he had accepted on trust. He remembered the old motto, *nullius in verba* (on the word of no one). Had it been a mistake not to question the veracity of the information? Just because it came from one's own side did not mean it was true.

He was not going to be a passive bystander in events. He may not have made the right decisions so far, but he could still turn things around and get them on the right track. An idea was slowly evolving in his mind, but he needed a concrete plan of action. Without one, the idea would amount to nothing.

He would go down to the records department and do some research of his own. He glanced at his watch. It was too late to go now, but he did have access to the Stonebridge report on his office computer. He felt better now that he had decided on his first step of action.

However, he would have to be careful. It was a dangerous thing to try and be too clever. You only ended up outsmarting yourself. You had to give your adversary credit but not too much.

Margaret came back into the room.

"That was Susan. She's running a bit late."

"Oh, I completely forgot she was coming."

No doubt she had run out of money, Anderson thought. Not that he minded giving her more. He had enough and knew she was at an age when it was easy to spend. How different it would have been if he had had a son. He loved his daughter, but there were always long uncomfortable silences between them when neither had anything to say. She was so much closer to her mother, but that was only natural.

"I suppose the roast is for her. You know you can't mother her all her life."

"I just want to make sure she gets something filling to eat. All that students live off are takeaways. There's nothing like a homemade dinner."

"How long is she staying for?"

"Just a few days."

"I'm going to have to pop into the office."

"Now?"

"It won't be for long. I need to check something."

"Can't it wait till morning?"

"I won't be long. I'll be back in time for dinner."

Margaret's face sagged with disappointment.

"OK," she said. "It's just that we spend so little time together—the three of us—like it used to be."

Anderson walked over to her and kissed her affectionately on the forehead. She looked up at him in surprise.

"I promise, I'll be back in time," Anderson said.

23

The offices were closing, tired workers spilling out onto the pavements. Emily emerged from Regent's Park station, made her way down Portland Place and stopped outside the six-storey embassy at the junction with Weymouth Street. The traffic ground to a halt as the lights changed to red and pedestrians hurried across.

The façade of the embassy's ground floor was painted white, whilst the upper floors were brown brick. The original embassy had been built in the eighteenth century but was demolished in 1980, on condition that the new building—which was completed in 1985—had the same façade—except with one entrance instead of the original two.

It was a common myth, Emily mused, that the Chinese did not have a word in their language for innovation but instead used the word copy. Even so, it was a culture that was second to none when it came to imitation, and of that, the embassy was an indisputable example.

Emily walked between the two white Doric pillars into the portico above which a red flag with its five gold stars fluttered. Patiently, she stood in front of the black door, the red, circular national emblem of the People's Republic of China etched on the transom window. She looked directly into the CCTV camera perched in the top right corner of the entrance; her distorted reflection spread over its convex lens. The buzzer sounded, and the door lock clicked open.

She stepped into the entrance hall. It was a cold and uninviting place with white walls and black polished marble flooring. On the grey tiled roof were several spotlights. It was a place that set the tone for the rest of the building. History and authority hung in the air. Before her, there were two mahogany doors. Between them, a large framed monochrome painting depicting several waterfalls.

The distant tapping of a keyboard could be heard emanating from behind the right-hand door. She walked up to it, her heels tapping on the hard floor, pushed it open, and entered the main lobby. Unlike the hall, this area was carpeted and reminded her of a cosy boutique hotel.

A solitary, effeminate man wearing a grey *Zhongshan* suit stood behind a counter tapping at a keyboard. He abruptly stopped as Emily entered. His expression remained fixed and inscrutable as she approached.

He glanced up at the clock on the wall.

"You are three minutes late. Mr Han is waiting for you in the meeting room."

Emily made no response.

"Through that door," he said, pointing to the far side of the room. "The first door on your right."

The first door was a polished oak double door with a gold plate: Meeting Room.

Emily knocked.

"Come in," a voice said.

The room was long and rectangular, with a thick beige carpet adorned with traditional Chinese designs. On the walls were various calligraphy and paintings by masters such as Qi Baishi and Xu Beihong. A horseshoe of red leather sofas lined the room. Sitting in the far corner was a small, wiry man, wearing round wire-rimmed glasses and a grey *Zhongshan* suit. Emily judged him to be about forty-five.

"Please sit down," the man said, his diction precise. "My name is Qi Han."

Emily watched him closely and sat down on the nearest sofa.

"Would you like something to drink? Tea?"

"No," Emily said, shaking her head. "I want to get on with this."

Han smiled and said, "This is not something that gives you satisfaction?"

"I'm doing this because I want my father released—no other reason."

Han's face twisted with cruel amusement.

"Be thankful the motherland has taken it upon herself to help him with his rehabilitation."

Emily glanced around the room. Her eyes fixed on a small statue of Mao on the mantelpiece. It was probably bugged and the reason for the man's obsequious manner. Even so, he was laying it on a bit thick. It wouldn't do him any good, Emily thought. His career path would be limited to the lower echelons of power. Obsequiousness was a good trait in a lackey but not in someone who wielded authority.

Han said, "Did you have any difficulty getting Taylor out of the hospital?"

Emily was fully aware that Han already knew what had happened. This was all part of a tried and tested routine to gauge her responses. To get a benchmark against which they—those controlling Han—would measure responses to questions for which they did not have answers.

It was possible that an infrared detector was measuring her body's heat signature. She looked up at a small ventilation panel but could see only darkness behind its grills.

She said, "Belakovsky tried to eliminate him."

"So, the Russians know. What happened to Belakovsky?"

"He killed himself."

"And Taylor? He was not injured?"

"No."

"Where is he now?"

"In a safe place."

"Have you implemented the mind sieve?"

"Yes."

"And he took it freely?"

"I told him that we used to work together."

"Oh? And that was all it took to convince him to take it?"

"Yes. He wants to know who he is. Wouldn't you?"

Han smiled and said, "And what did he tell you?"

Emily paused as she took a moment to think.

"He told me his name is Bruce Taylor."

"And *who* is Bruce Taylor?"

"He was part of an elite surveillance team which targeted Chinese agents for a programme called Clean Start."

"Details, please."

Emily took a small USB drive from her pocket and placed it on the table.

"Everything's on this," she said.

Han picked up the drive and examined it.

"I would still prefer it if you gave me a summary."

Emily recapitulated what she had told Taylor. When she finished, Han arched an eyebrow.

"That was all he told you about Clean Start? You didn't find out what happened to him at Stonebridge?"

"No. The mind sieve couldn't penetrate those memories."

"I see. You will have to excuse me for a moment."

Han got to his feet and left through a side door. Emily patiently waited, conscious that she was being watched. Five minutes later, Han returned and seated himself.

"I have new instructions for you."

"No, I've done my part. I want to see my father."

"Your job is not finished. We need to know more about what happened at Stonebridge."

Burning anger rising in her, Emily said, "I've done everything that was asked of me. I implemented the mind sieve. If it couldn't find out what you wanted to know, that's not my fault. Let me speak to someone in authority."

Han bristled.

"I am your contact here. You will talk to me and me alone."

"You're just a puppet on a string. I want to talk to whoever is pulling your strings."

Emily got to her feet.

Han said, "This behaviour is inexcusable. You must—"

He abruptly stopped as the telephone on the table rang. He nervously glanced across at the small statue of Mao, and a weak smile creased his lips.

"You will excuse me," he said calmly.

He picked up the phone. Speaking in Mandarin, he repeatedly bowed in response to what he was told. Colour rose in his face, and finally, he replaced the receiver.

He took a moment to compose himself before saying, "I am sure we can keep matters civil. There is no need for emotions to get out of control. It is undignified."

He held out his hand, indicating the sofa, and said, "Please."

Emily sat down.

"You will have your wish to see your father."

Emily's face lit up.

"Now? He's here?"

"Not quite. But once you have done what we expect of you, you will be allowed to see him."

A chill ran down Emily's back.

"You are to take Bruce Taylor to Beijing."

"Beijing! That was not what I agreed to."

"That is where your father is. If you wish to see him, you must comply with this new arrangement. The mind sieve is not the only means we have of helping people remember. Back in the motherland, we have much more advanced techniques, but they require a greater length of time—something we do not have the luxury of here with the police and government agents searching for Taylor."

"How am I supposed to get him out of the country? The police have put out an APW."

"We will assist with the necessary documentation."

"And how do I convince him to go?"

"You persuaded him to take the mind sieve. I'm sure you will find a way. You are a very resourceful young lady. However, if you do not feel up to it, I am sure someone can be found who will take over from you."

Han smiled.

Emily, ashen-faced, her eyes downcast, said, "No, I'll do it."

"Good. You will go back to reception, where you will be given an envelope that will contain your new instructions.

"There is no reason to be unhappy. The motherland is bending over backwards for you. You should consider it a great honour to be of such use."

"Are you finished?"

"Yes," Han said, nodding.

Emily got to her feet and left the room.

Back in reception, she was handed an envelope sealed with red wax, bearing the image of the Chinese dragon. The receptionist stood, impassively watching her.

"You will not open it now. Be sure you are alone when you read it."

Emily slipped the envelope into her pocket and left.

As a child, Emily had watched a TV documentary that included archive footage of the then British Prime Minister, Edward Heath, on a guided tour of China, talking with a former dissident who had undergone re-education.

"Now, I understand," the released dissident had said.

Emily stood in the crowded carriage of the underground train staring at her reflection in the window, thinking about the dissident, the monotonous clatter of the steel wheels on the rails filling the carriage.

He had been in his early sixties and looked close to death, his loose jacket hanging off his thin, frail body. What had horrified Emily the most were his vacant eyes which peered out from sunken sockets. There was a look of total defeat in them. He was only a man in name.

He talked to the Prime Minister about how he had been wrong to criticise the government—that he had been ill, and now he understood the error of his ways. He wanted only forgiveness and the chance to redeem himself.

He was, Emily mused, so broken that he would quite happily have told the Prime Minister that one plus one was three. Or anything else the party machinery wanted him to say. And not just say it but believe it.

Right now, her father was being subjected to re-education. They would break him down, just as they had the dissident, strip him of his personality and rebuild him to suit their purposes. The thought sickened her. If she did not act and deliver Taylor to Beijing, she knew with absolute certainty that she would, after many years, when he was finally released, hear her father say those ominous words: now, I understand. And he would look at her, as though she were a stranger, through dead eyes.

24

Thames House (MI5 HQ), situated at the corner of Millbank and Horseferry Road, was a building which always filled Anderson with nostalgia for a past he had only ever experienced vicariously through the stories his father had recounted to him of his service in Delhi as British Ambassador during the Raj.

The imperial neoclassical design gave more than a nod to Edwin Lutyens, who had designed large swathes of Delhi during the twenties and thirties. Standing in the chill evening air, Anderson thought of the sweltering heat of India and the long, lazy days his father spent playing polo and attending garden parties. By his own admission, Anderson was as prone as the next person to romanticise about that period of British history, especially when he looked up at the impressive Portland Stone façade inscribed with numerous coats of arms and Latin mottos. It was a building that belonged to an empire, not some small and increasingly insignificant island in the North Sea.

Across the still, black waters of the Thames, the obelisk that was the Millbank Tower rose high above the surrounding buildings, its minimalist sixties design in stark contrast to the ornate architecture of Thames House. The only thing which stood out about the Millbank Tower was its sheer size, measuring over a hundred metres high. Anderson felt there was nothing of lasting value in its simple design.

A few lights shone out from it; most of the staff had long since finished their day's work. Anderson could see the stooping outline of a cleaner high up on the twentieth floor pushing a vacuum cleaner under a desk. Farther down the river, the Palace of Westminster, lit up with spotlights, seemed to float above the Thames, its perfect reflection caught in the black waters.

The wind picked up as it ushered in a fierce torrent of rain. The waters of the Thames came to life, the reflection of Millbank Tower and parliament instantly transformed into a blur of orange light in the rippling waters.

Anderson broke into a half run, stopping when he was safely under the archway of Thames House. He brushed himself off and walked in. A uniformed security guard was sitting at the front desk, a row of six screens by his elbow. His inscrutable face showed no emotion as Anderson handed him his ID card.

Anderson saw no one as he made his way up to his office. Behind several half-open doors, he heard vacuum cleaners and saw half-filled black rubbish bags. There was no one in the outer office. There were several Post-it notes on his secretary's computer monitor, most of which related to shopping.

He went into his office, seated himself behind his desk, turned on the lamp, and logged in to his computer. He pulled over the keyboard and mouse, moving the cursor over the icon of an X. He would start from the beginning: Stonebridge.

His part in the Stonebridge investigation had been to arrange the bugging of the mansion. It was not a successful endeavour, yielding nothing of value. Brenner, the Australian industrialist, who was the focus of the investigation, would undoubtedly have assumed that he was under surveillance. During the whole op until its abrupt end, Anderson's team had recorded hundreds of hours of classical music and mundane conversations between Brenner and his kitchen staff about the menu for the various functions held at the mansion. At first, his team had thought it was some kind of code but later concluded that Brenner was simply playing them, well aware of the presence of the bugs.

The key point of interest about Brenner was how he had transformed a small electronics company into a powerful multinational in such a short space of time. It had gone from a small start-up to a major player in the lucrative software sector within two years. No loans had been taken from any banks, and the company was not listed on any stock exchange. The company's finances were shrouded in secrecy, and—as much as the intelligence services dug—they found nothing incriminating.

They knew the Russians were funding the company but did not know how so much currency was being transferred into the country. Various back channels were investigated, and it was assumed that bitcoins were the primary source of financing, although, without concrete evidence, this remained just a theory. Soon, Brenner International acquired majority stake holdings in important multinationals, some of which were involved in government contracts.

Anderson double-clicked the X icon and entered his password at the prompt. A hierarchical directory of files filled the screen. He selected the Stonebridge file and opened it. The Stonebridge dossier's cover page filled the screen. He clicked the mouse and moved onto the inside pages that, to his surprise, were all heavily redacted. Sentences and even entire paragraphs had been blacked out. He scrolled through the following pages and found all had been similarly redacted.

He had the highest security clearance level; there was no reason he should be looking at a version of the file intended for junior staff.

He closed the window and then repeated the rigmarole of the logging-in procedure, opening the file again only to find himself staring at the same redacted document.

He stared perplexedly at the screen, at a complete loss. If it was a problem with the system, he knew there was nothing he could do to resolve it; he was, for all intents and purposes, IT illiterate, and he would have to leave it till the morning to get his hands on the unredacted version of the file. Annoyed, he closed the window and turned his attention to the personnel icon on his desktop. He clicked it and navigated through the various menus until he found the personnel file belonging to Anne Richmond.

The cover page was a standard contact form consisting of personal details. In the top corner, a photograph, a green watermark running horizontally across it.

He began reading the file in earnest. It covered both her time with MI5 and GCHQ. Her record with MI5 was that of an outstanding officer. Based on what he read, it was clear that she had been destined for big things. However, her transfer and effective demotion to GCHQ had seemingly put an end to her prospects. She had taken what was essentially a junior, entry-level job as part of a team translating Russian Intelligence. Strange, Anderson thought, how she had simply faded into the shadows. What would make someone throw away their career at such a young age?

He scrolled back to her photograph and studied it. He gave no credence to physiognomy, but he could not help but form an opinion about the face in the photograph. There was, he felt, a trace of melancholy in those soft feminine features. Her eyes seemed dead, lustreless. Or am I seeing what I want to see? Anderson thought. He hadn't seen these qualities before he had started reading. Why should he see them now? Unless that was, he had been influenced by what he had read? Even so, something had happened to her, something bad.

He scrolled back up to the contact page. She was twenty-eight and lived in a flat in Cheltenham. She was married, but an asterisk had been scribbled, in pen, against this entry. Anderson glanced at the bottom of the page for a related footnote, but there was none. He rapidly scrolled through pages looking for other footnotes but reached the end of the file and found no explanation for the asterisk. No doubt, he thought, that the scanning assistant had omitted the relevant page when the file had been transferred from the original paper copy.

He closed the file and, after another quick navigation of the directory, found Bruce Taylor's file. The only update in the past three years was the entry for his status: ACTIVE was crossed out and updated to DECEASED. As he had done with Anne, Anderson took a moment to consider the photograph on the contact page. It was a bland, uninteresting face, a face you would not look at twice if you saw it on the street. That was a good quality, Anderson thought. Being noticed, being remembered was the worst thing that could happen to an officer—an assassin.

He blinked, leant forward in his seat and involuntarily ran his hand across the screen. He glanced across at the desk lamp and then back at the screen. There was no doubt about it. The watermark running across the photograph was the same pale green as in Anne's. However, the green watermark had only been used for the past year. Before that, a red one had been used, and that was what should have been on Taylor's photograph.

Had the file been tampered with? Was there an innocent explanation that he was overlooking? The watermark's colour may have been no more than an aberration from when the file had been digitised. Or they may have updated the photograph when the file had been scanned. To Anderson, these explanations sounded contrived.

The only way to be sure about the colour of the watermark and know whether the file had been altered would be to see the original paper copy. That would have to wait until morning when the records department opened.

25

There had been a time after her husband's death when Anne had thought she would never care deeply about anything or anyone ever again, including herself. She had considered the rest of her life as just playing out time.

It is often said that one can find a silver lining in any situation or that when one door closes, another opens. But not for Anne. The only thing which gave her life meaning was gone. They had been in love—truly in love. She never felt, with him, that there would be a time when they would have grown too familiar with each other. She loved him as much on the last day she had seen him as the day she had first fallen for him.

In over five years as an MI5 officer, she had been to many homicide scenes. The cordons, the pathologist examining the body, teams of forensic technicians gathering evidence and body bags were a familiar sight to her. Hence, the dead bodies of the Cartwrights had not made a profound impression on her. However, until today, she had never witnessed the moment the spark of life was extinguished.

It seemed absurd to her how the panic-stricken Woodstein had simply stepped away from the wall, and in an instant, his life had been snuffed out for all eternity. She had always imagined that moment of human death as being something momentous. But it was as meaningless and inconsequential as in a mindless action movie.

She did not blame herself for his death. Playing back the events in her mind, she would not have acted any differently. Woodstein had lost control, and there was nothing she could have done. One moment he was a living, breathing person and the next, a corpse.

Anne took a sip from her lukewarm tea. For over thirty minutes, she had been sitting watching a costume drama on TV with the volume muted. Without the distraction of music and dialogue, there was something absurd about grown men and women, dressed as sultans and courtesans, their faces blackened, strutting about the stage.

In the immediate aftermath of Woodstein's death, she had been so pumped full of adrenaline that she had thought of nothing except what to do next. The training had stepped in, and all instinctive human emotions had been pushed to the back of her mind. Now she was suffering from an acute stress reaction as her mind tried to process what she had seen and come to terms with how close she had come to ending up like Woodstein. She had never had a set routine for dealing with stress. Even though she had undergone a battery of psychological tests when she had joined MI5, she was still as susceptible to stress as any person off the street. Over the years, she had been instructed in various techniques, including mindfulness meditation and yoga. The doctors had assured her they would help her deal with stressful situations. They did not.

She thought of her husband. Had it been quick and painless for him as it had been for Woodstein? She hoped it had. When she had been notified of his death, she had refused to identify his body, preferring instead to read the coroner's report. When his body had been pulled out of the river, it had been covered in livid bruises. He had been beaten with a blunt object, which the pathologist had concluded was probably a hammer. His nails had been torn from his fingers, several teeth had been pulled out, his ears cut off, and his shaven head scorched with an acetylene torch. She had always clung to the hope that his body had been mutilated, for effect, after being murdered.

Shortly after his death, she heard rumours of a training programme that could permanently eradicate feelings of guilt and depression and completely rejuvenate worn-out officers. She had seriously considered signing up but had, at the last minute, changed her mind. It was not a character flaw to feel the way she did, and perversely, she wanted to keep suffering, as if only by doing so could she keep his memory alive. She was afraid that if the pain faded and ceased—if she moved on with her life—it would be as if she had stopped loving him.

However, her immediate priority had been to keep her job; she could not cope with financial insecurity on top of everything else. She had to keep her feelings hidden. It would not look good on her record if she admitted to being depressed. Like most other officers, she had to endure bouts of nervous tension in silence. There was a high percentage of officers who were secret drinkers and drug addicts.

She started at the sound of a loud rap on the front door. Getting up, she put her cup of tea on the table and went into the hallway. Through the door's obscure glass panel, she could see the dark outline of a small man.

Opening the door, she blinked, momentarily lost for words.

"Anne, I hope I haven't caught you at an inconvenient time?" Charters said.

The light from the flat above gave his face a sickly orange pallor.

"No, please come in, sir."

As Anne took a step back, allowing Charters to enter, a sudden gust of wind blew across his face.

"Ghastly weather," he said. "I can't remember the last time it wasn't raining."

"Please go straight through."

Charters did as bid, and Anne followed him into the living room.

"Nice place, very cosy."

"Would you like something to drink?"

Charters looked down at the half-empty cup of tea.

"I've got a bottle of whisky in the kitchen," Anne said.

Charters smiled.

"I see my reputation precedes me. No, thank you. But something warm to get the heat back into my head would be nice. A cup of tea—if it's no problem."

"Not at all. Please, sit down."

Anne went into the kitchen; Charters took off his wet raincoat, looked around for a place to hang it, but finding none, folded it up and put it on a chair. He looked at the TV and then glanced around the room and nodded, satisfied that everything was as he had expected. He slowly lowered himself onto the sofa.

Anne came back into the room holding a mug of tea, a bowl of sugar and a small carton of cream. She placed them on the low coffee table.

"I'm sorry, I don't know how you take it, sir."

"No, please. I can manage."

Charters leant over and proceeded to empty the carton of cream into his tea, followed by three heaped teaspoons of sugar.

"I've got a *very* sweet tooth," he said. "My GP thinks sugar's the root of all evil and is responsible for the obesity epidemic. You know, he once told me that he would never eat a pear. 'Water and sugar,' he said. 'There's no nutritional value in it.'

I said, 'What about eating for pleasure?' He looked at me as if I'd lost my mind. How can you take anything a man like that says seriously?"

Anne picked up the remote control on the table and turned off the TV.

"I just put it on to help me unwind," she said.

"Yes. I've been briefed about what happened."

"Any news on the assassin?"

"No. We're working on a few leads. At least we know it's the Chinese we're dealing with and not the Russians."

"And Woodstein? Was he married?"

"No immediate family. You've lived here a long time?"

"Six years."

"With your husband?"

"I'm … I'm not married."

Charters arched an eyebrow. Anne began fidgeting with her hands.

"I'm a widow."

"Oh, I'm sorry."

"It's been a year. Sam worked for D Branch. He was infiltrating a drug cartel when his cover got blown. They found his body floating in the Volga."

"Is that why you transferred?"

"Yes. I took a few months off. Looking back, it was the worst thing I could've done. I had too much time to think and go over things in my head. I kept remembering the last time I saw him. I wish—"

Anne abruptly stopped and looked up at Charters, who was leaning forward, listening intently.

"I'm sorry, sir. I didn't mean to go on."

"Don't be. Being human is not something for which you should ever apologise. It's reassuring to know that we don't employ robots."

"When I heard what they'd done to him, I wanted to kill them all."

"And now?"

"I don't know. It wouldn't change anything; it wouldn't bring him back."

Charters took a sip from his tea and said, "This is good."

He put down the cup and added, "I want to send you out on another op. But it's not one for which I can give you any support. You'll be operating alone."

"Is it officially sanctioned by GCHQ?"

"You've been with us a long time. I don't need to tell you that sometimes we have to operate outside the envelope of what's legal. The rules of the game are always changing, and we can't sit and wait for the politicians to legislate before we can act. So, to answer your question: no. It's not sanctioned by GCHQ, SIS or MI5. There'll be no record it ever happened."

"Sir, why are you asking me?"

"Stonebridge is still raising sand all these years on. You're one of the few people who know about Taylor's reappearance. The fewer people I can bring into the loop, the better. More to the point, you speak Russian, and it's to Russia I want to send you."

"What's the op?"

"I can't tell you anything until you decide whether to accept. All I can tell you is that it is dangerous. I can't guarantee your safety. If things go wrong, you'll have to find your own way out. Given what you've told me about your husband, I'll understand if you say no. I won't hold it against you.

"If you succeed, I'll personally see to it that you can get your old job back—a promotion too. I know you're not motivated by career or money. It's just a way I have of showing my appreciation should you accept."

Without any hesitation, Anne said, "I'll do it."

26

The sun broke through the cloud cover; the morning mist had cleared, and the bright sunlight sparkled off the dew-moist leaves of the oak trees that lined the street.

Anderson took in the sights and sounds of the morning rush hour. The familiar aroma of fried pork and relish from a hot dog stand, the honking of car horns, and the faces of office workers all flashed past him. He arrived for work half an hour earlier than usual. His secretary looked up in surprise as he entered the outer office.

"Stephanie, get me John Sanders on the phone."

"Yes, sir."

"How's my diary looking?"

"Routine meetings, nothing important. I've put a copy on your desk."

"OK. Do you know what time they start in the records department?"

"Oh, they started an hour ago."

Anderson went into his office and took a cursory look at his schedule for the day.

It was good to be back in his familiar office. It had been an uncomfortable evening. With Margaret busy in the kitchen, he had found himself alone with his daughter in the dining room. There had been long uncomfortable silences between the two of them, just as he had feared, with him looking down at his plate and playing with his food. She had only been gone a year, but she had changed, grown up in that time. He hadn't expected that. Although she hadn't exactly been all elbows and knees when she had left, she had matured quickly and was now a woman—gone was his little girl.

It was evident from what she said that she had the intensity of conviction typical in young intellectuals. He hadn't wanted to get into a deep philosophical discussion and got the feeling from what she said that she wouldn't look too favourably on what he did. She sounded very idealistic. God, Anderson thought, she could even be a communist. They were as active as they had been in the sixties—recruiting in universities.

He was immensely relieved when dinner was over, and he could retire for the night. Even though he had had eight hours of sleep, he awoke, feeling bilious. Throughout the night, his mind had worked subconsciously to resolve the issues which had arisen regarding the redacted Stonebridge file and Taylor's tampered personnel photograph.

The phone on his desk rang, and he grabbed the receiver.

"Yes?"

"Sanders," the voice answered.

"Sanders. A week ago—the twenty-first—there was an incident in Haylesbury. A tramp got into a fight and was arrested. Pull the police report and send it to me."

"Do you want me to go through official channels?"

"No. No one's to know about this."

"That's going to take time. How soon do you need it?

"ASAP."

"I'll see what I can do."

Anderson put down the receiver and left his office.

The lift came to a soft halt as it reached the lower ground floor. The doors slid apart, and Anderson stepped into a corridor lit by soft-tone spotlights. There was a yucca plant on a small table, and a hard-tiled floor led to an open carpeted space with a stained reading desk in the corner. Anderson was reminded of the waiting area in a GP's surgery.

Opposite the desk was a circular counter, behind which were rows of shelves crammed full of files. An elderly woman was seated at the counter. Her face a deathly white due to the overapplication of makeup and years spent in this subterranean world. She looked up and blinked as Anderson approached.

"Mr Anderson," she said in surprise.

A couple of heads peered out from behind the shelves.

Anderson felt like royalty descending to meet the common people. He knew the staff would talk about this for weeks afterwards. It was usual for files to be requested and then sent up, but seldom, if ever, did someone from the top echelons of the organisation ever come down. Indeed, this was the first time Anderson had been here.

"I need a few files."

"Of course, sir."

The woman pushed a small notepad across the counter.

"If you would fill in the details."

Anderson scribbled down Stonebridge, Anne Richmond and Bruce Taylor.

The woman examined the page and turned around.

"William."

A young man wearing a thick woollen sweater and glasses with lenses as thick as bottle ends emerged from behind the bookshelf. The woman tore off the page, handed it to him, and he disappeared between the shelves.

"The Stonebridge file is kept separate. It's only available for viewing in the reading room. If you would follow me, sir."

The woman emerged from behind the counter, and Anderson followed her to a side room. It was windowless, ten feet square, furnished with a metal table and chair, overlooked by a CCTV camera. Covering an entire wall were turquoise safe deposit boxes, small number plates on each one.

The woman said, "Box 1618. I'll be outside if you require any assistance."

"Do you have access to the boxes?"

"No, everything in this room is classified to Level 5."

"I see. I'll call you if I need anything."

The woman left.

Anderson looked up and down the rows of boxes. They were sequentially ordered; he found number 1618 in the middle. Each box had a small scanner, and he pressed his thumb against 1618's.

There followed, almost instantaneously, a click as the lock released. He pulled back the door, drew out the long rectangular steel box and pushed back the lid. His breathing became quick and shallow. The box was empty.

A cold sweat broke over his forehead. He turned and glanced up at the CCTV camera and then slammed shut the box. His legs felt weak, his head light. He double-checked the number on the box. It was 1618—no doubt about it. He put the box back in its slot, closed the door and left the room.

Behind the counter, the woman was in a heated discussion with William.

"Check again," she demanded. "It must be there."

She broke off when she saw Anderson. William disappeared between the shelves.

To Anderson, the woman said, "Do you need something, sir?"

143

"Is there a problem?"

"I'm sorry, sir. The files you requested seem to have been mislaid."

"Both of them?"

"It would appear so. Are you finished with the Stonebridge file?"

"Yes, do you know if anyone else has asked to see it?"

"No one, sir."

"You're sure?"

"Positive. I can check the logbook, if you like?"

"Please."

The woman pulled out a thick volume from beneath the counter and started leafing through it.

"No one in the past six months," she said. "Do you want me to check further back?"

Anderson's phone rang. He took it out from his jacket pocket and glanced at the caller ID. It was Sanders. He pressed the green answer button.

"Sanders, what have you got?"

"Nothing."

"What do you mean?"

"There was no incident in Haylesbury on the date you gave me. I checked a week on either side as well—nothing. And it seems I wasn't the only one who was curious. DCI Hall has been making enquiries."

"OK, thanks."

Anderson hung up and, having lost his train of thought, stared at the woman.

"Do you want me to check further back?" she asked.

"No, no. If it turns up, let me know."

"I will, sir. Once again, I'm very sorry. We'll conduct a thorough search and send up the files once they've been located."

Anderson went back to the lift, stabbed the button and waited. The doors parted. Charters stood before him.

He stepped out, put his hand on Anderson's shoulder and said, "I think we need to talk."

27

Taylor watched the news report with interest. DCI Hall was standing outside Mountview hospital, surrounded by TV crews.

In answer to a journalist's question, Hall said. "I can confirm that three members of staff were murdered yesterday morning. All were foreign nationals, and we're still in the process of contacting their next of kin. We'll release more details in due course, but at present, we're still following up various lines of enquiry, and it would be inappropriate for me to comment further."

Taylor turned off the TV and went over to the window. It had been two hours since Emily had left. He had gone over again and again what the mind sieve had unearthed, but he could still find no emotional connection to the man she had told him he had been. He still thought of Bruce Taylor as someone else, driven by motives and desires that no longer existed.

Emily's car turned the corner and pulled up in front of the house. She killed the engine and sat for a moment, staring ahead, seemingly oblivious to the world around her. Her face was drawn, her eyes bleak. The look sent a wave of despondency through Taylor, and he knew things had not gone well.

Emily composed herself, got out of the car, and went into the house.

"Did you make contact?" Taylor asked, coming down the stairs as Emily closed the front door.

"Oh," Emily said, slightly disoriented. "You've shaved? You look so much younger."

"This is how I used to look?"

146

"Yes."

"How did the meeting go?"

"Let's talk about it inside."

Taylor stepped up to her and took her hands in his.

"You're cold," he said. "I'll get some coffee."

He made his way into the kitchen. Emily took off her coat and went into the living room. A minute later, Taylor entered, holding a coffee which Emily gratefully took, shuddering as she took a satisfying gulp. She sat down on the sofa and wrapped her hands around the mug.

"Things have got more complicated. I can't bring you in."

"Why not?"

"They want us to go to Beijing. They've got a network in place there."

"Beijing! You did tell them that I don't remember anything."

"They know. They got your medical records from the hospital."

"Then what use am I to them? This makes no sense."

"They don't give reasons, just orders. Some analyst or strategist has decided that you can be of use to them there."

"Who did you talk to?"

"John Evans. You used to work together."

Taylor slowly shook his head.

"I don't remember him. He just expects me to do what I'm told?"

"They won't help you unless you help them."

"Do they want me to kill someone?"

"I don't know. It's a possibility."

Taylor's sat down, stared intensely at Emily and said, "What if we disappeared?"

"What?"

"What if we ran, went somewhere they couldn't find us."

"Where would we go?"

"I don't know. We could find somewhere—start over. I don't want to be the man I was. I don't want to come in if this is the price."

"They'll come after you. You'll be marked as a security risk, and they won't think twice about eliminating you or me. Remember, they want me to go as well."

"Will you?"

"I don't have a choice. I knew the deal when I was recruited. After it's all over, they'll bring you in. Evans gave me his word."

"And you believe him?"

"It doesn't matter. What choice do we have?"

"They're like blackmailers trying to squeeze every last drop out of us. They'll always ask for more—this will never end."

"It's a risk I have to take. If you want to run, that's your call."

"You're going?"

"I have to."

"Why do you 'have to'?"

Emily got to her feet and turned her back to Taylor.

"I can't say."

Taylor stood up, put his hands on her shoulder and said, "What's this hold they've got over you?"

"Don't ask me. Just believe me when I tell you that I have to go. I don't have a choice."

"Then neither do I."

Emily turned around.

"I left you once before," Taylor said. "I won't do it again."

"You deserve more than this. You're such a good man."

"A good man who's killed people."

28

"Do you play?" Charters asked, standing over the chessboard in his office.

His office was spacious with an expensive Persian rug, thick green curtains—sunlight filtered through the windows onto the hardwood floor and the flowery William Morris wallpaper. There was an antique George IV Partners desk with an immaculate black hide lining and a mahogany shelf filled with thick Moroccan bound volumes.

The Doughnut may have been modern, but Charters had a fixed view about how an executive's office should look. The office would have been more in keeping with Thames House's classical architecture.

Anderson glanced at the chessboard on the stained walnut table. The position was an endgame with only a few pieces left.

"Not very well. I know how the pieces move."

"My opponent isn't very good, but he's getting better. He's got me in quite a pickle at the moment. There're a lot of similarities between chess and real life. The position looks relatively simple, with only a few pieces left, yet, the number of possible moves is mind-boggling.

"In any position, you must have a plan. Only then can you think about executing it. The best players can disguise their strategy. Before you know it, you're under attack from two fronts, and defence is impossible. But I'm going off into the abstract. Let's talk details."

"About Stonebridge?"

Charters smiled.

"Yes. Stonebridge," he said.

He walked over to his desk, pulled open a drawer and took out a thick dossier tied together with treasury tags—stamped on its cover, in capitals: STONEBRIDGE.

He dropped it on his desk and said, "You've always been too conscientious. This was what you were looking for. The file on the system has been tagged; it sends me an alert whenever it's accessed."

"The version on the system has been redacted."

Charters patted the dossier and said, "Yes. This is the full, clean copy."

"And the files for Richmond and Taylor?"

"They're in a safe place."

"Why?"

"Prudence. I don't want things to get too complicated. As with chess, I like to keep the play simple. How much do you know about Stonebridge?"

"Not as much as I'd like or hoped to."

Charters chuckled.

"Then, let me fill you in. It's been a long time. We're still not sure how Brenner got out of the country. Intelligence believes that he was probably smuggled aboard a plane in diplomatic baggage. He is a small man, so it's not as far-fetched as it sounds.

"But there were things more important than the man. In many ways, it didn't matter what happened to him. He was just a tool the Russians used. However, it was acutely embarrassing for us when he was paraded on Russian TV like some kind of trophy. The Foreign Office is still smarting over the whole affair.

"We're still patchy about how he managed to get the finances from his controllers and how he managed to infiltrate other companies to acquire their industrial secrets."

"But that was never the main focus of the inquiry we had after his escape, was it?"

"No. The question has always been whether he had help."

"Did he?"

"I'm ninety-nine per cent certain he did. But we still don't know who? The view has always been that it was more than one person—a team.

"Taylor was en route to Stonebridge to eliminate Brenner when he disappeared. We were restricted in any follow-up investigation, given that he was part of an illegal assassination programme. But it's not this fact alone, which means we must stop any of this getting out. Do you know what we did to them? How we turned them into such efficient killers?"

A cold chill ran down Anderson's spine.

"No," he said.

"You could pick almost any man—or woman, for that matter—out of a crowd and train him to become an assassin. The assassins of Clean Start didn't have any specialist skills. All the necessary weapons training and close-quarters combat skills could have been acquired on any training programme. On Clean Start, they underwent a unique treatment programme. What we had by the end of it were assassins who would kill anyone designated for assassination, and most importantly, with a complete lack of empathy.

"The treatment programme was the brainchild of Dr Charles Henley, a maverick expert in the field of neuroscience and, in particular, DBS (Deep Brain Stimulation). Much of the work in this field had been developed by the CIA during their

MKUltra parapsychology programme. As you know, that ran for about twenty years in secret up until the mid-seventies. Unwitting subjects were experimented upon, often with disastrous outcomes.

"No one was ever brought to book over its unethical practices, and most of the research proved useless, but some did yield interesting results. DBS was one of them.

"It works by drilling into the brain of a patient and inserting electrodes. These are powered by a battery that is secreted in the chest cavity. Once activated, the electrodes stimulate the brain, firing off neurons.

"It was found to be useful in treating diseases such as Parkinson's and chronic pains which result from misfiring neurons.

"In the cases of Parkinson's, the uncontrollable tremors stopped immediately once the battery was switched on. DBS was a significant breakthrough.

"When we acquired the detailed notes of MKUltra, one question arose. Was it possible to use DBS not just to stop misfiring neurons that caused physical pain but to stop them firing up the parts of the brain responsible for feelings of guilt? If such an outcome were possible, it would give our black op units a distinct advantage, officers who could act without remorse or feelings of guilt, no matter how unsavoury the task they had been given.

"Within our previous elimination units, there'd always been a high rate of mental breakdown. We went along the route they did in America with their marines, training them so that they saw the enemy as less than human, someone not deserving of any compassion or mercy. It worked, but once they got back to civilian life, they couldn't just turn off their training. Domestic abuse rates soared, and after several high-profile murders, they had to change their approach. Our new treatment proved to be a radical solution.

"Taylor underwent DBS?"

"Yes. Three people were recruited for the programme. They were all originally MI6 officers. But MI6 wouldn't transfer them to Clean Start unless we took joint responsibility. No one ever wants complete ownership of a black op in case of blowback if things go wrong. So, as you know, they were all technically GCHQ, MI6 and MI5 officers. We were going to bring in our own people and expand it if it proved a success. They knew what they would be asked to do, and they were never coerced.

"That doesn't make it any more ethical."

"Ethics are for dreamers. You know that. We live and work in the real world. We're the guardians, the ones who make it possible for people to sleep easy at night.

Anderson said nothing.

Charters continued, "Each had their own unique characteristic: Bruce Taylor suffered from crippling anxiety; Eve Stanton had a history of chronic depression; John Hunter had suffered a complete mental breakdown.

"Henley thought the fact that they had mental problems could actually be a benefit. They would be more willing to give up their old lives, and start afresh, make a clean start. Hence the name of the programme.

"Hunter was our most successful officer. He eliminated over twenty people without leaving a trace. All the deaths were accounted for by local law enforcement as being drugs-related."

"What happened to him and Stanton?"

"Stanton committed suicide; Hunter relapsed."

"What caused the relapse?"

"I think Henley's logic about using people with mental problems was flawed. Hunter's underlying problems persisted and, in the end, were too much for him. He had a total breakdown, became virtually catatonic.

"In hindsight, we overused him. Clean Start became an easy option. It was a lot simpler to eliminate enemy agents than have them put through the court system with all the negative publicity that involves."

"Where's he now?"

"Hunter?"

Charters looked down at his chessboard and pushed his King to the edge of the board.

"In a safe place."

"Are we going to revive Clean Start?"

"It's possible. We need to do more research. It depends as well on how this Taylor business pans out. The police have put out an APW for him?"

"Yes. Pritchard thinks there's a high possibility that he'll try to get out of the country.

"A fair assessment. Do you agree with him?"

"Yes."

"Let's hope this time he's made the right call. It didn't quite work out sending in Anne Richmond."

Anderson said nothing.

29

It was a busy evening in Heathrow Airport's Terminal Four. Glum, tired passengers lounged in departures drinking cups of coffee and eating sandwiches while bored children ran around trying to amuse themselves.

Taylor stood outside on the concourse, taking a long drag from his cigarette. He had no recollection of ever smoking, but it appeared he had, and he liked it, already having finished a packet. Emily emerged from a doorway and beckoned to him. He picked up his suitcase and went over to her.

"There's a long queue," he said.

"We're using the express check-in."

The two of them walked past a patrolling policeman, the radio, strapped to his body armour, blaring, a submachine gun tucked under his arm, his hand gripping tight its butt. There was no queue at the express check-in. Taylor hauled his luggage onto the conveyor belt. The Air China receptionist smiled.

Emily's instructions had been explicit; deviation from them would not be tolerated. The unsettling thought had occurred to her that they were being used as a decoy for another op. She knew enough about the workings of the Chinese Ministry of State Security (MSS) to know that they had many coals in the fire at any one time. This whole thing could be a setup, the price for someone else of more value being smuggled out of the country.

She glanced nervously around. At any moment, she expected a policeman's hand on her shoulder, followed by a command to follow him to a room where she and Taylor would be questioned. At least by avoiding the queues in economy class, they would not be standing about for an age. She would know soon enough whether the two of them were simply sacrificial lambs.

"Good evening," the receptionist said.

Taylor and Emily placed their passports on the counter. The smiling receptionist scooped them up, flicked open the front page of Taylor's passport and examined it. In a swift, deft movement, she slipped her hand under the counter and pressed a button. Another receptionist, dressed in an identical red uniform, emerged from a back office, took the two passports and disappeared back into the office.

The receptionist smiled and said, "Would you like a window seat?"

"We don't mind," Emily said.

"Any carry-on luggage?"

"No."

The receptionist tapped on her keyboard, and a printer spewed out a roll of paper. She ripped off the luggage tag and attached it to the bag on the conveyor belt. Her colleague emerged from the back office and handed her a manila envelope before once again going back into the office. The receptionist opened the envelope, which had been folded down but not sealed and took out two new passports.

She placed them on the counter together with two boarding passes.

"Seats 6A and 6B. Have an enjoyable flight."

Taylor gathered up the documents and headed for the border control.

He flipped open the front page of Emily's passport. Closing it, he handed it to her and said, "There's still an hour before the flight leaves, Miss Zhāng. Do you want something to eat or drink?"

Emily smiled.

"No, Mr Zhāng. It's better if we get security out of the way."

They walked on. Emily was filled with a feeling of euphoria. The first obstacle had been overcome. Abruptly, she stopped dead in her tracks. The snap of the safety being released from the machine gun was unmistakable. She turned to face the approaching policeman, his boots thudding on the hard stone floor, his face set and determined, pointing the barrel of his automatic weapon at Taylor.

"Don't move," he commanded.

Taylor glanced across the concourse. Two men in suits were running towards them.

They were taken to separate interview rooms. The one to which Taylor was taken had a pair of blue padded chairs on either side of a table. Taylor patiently waited for the man in the black suit who had escorted him to the room to return. Through the glass panel of the door, he could see the shadow of an armed policeman standing guard. It was not as if he were in any danger; they were all on the same side. When they made the necessary enquiries regarding his identity, MI5 would have no choice but to bring him in.

The door opened, and the black-suited man entered. Taylor guessed that he was in his early twenties, and from the excited look in his eyes, this was one of the first major incidents in his career. He carefully placed Taylor's passport on the table. Taylor glanced at it and then at the man.

"Would you like to be called Mr Zhāng or Mr Taylor? Or do you have any other names?"

"Taylor will do."

"OK, Taylor. There're a lot of people who want to talk to you: Scotland Yard, GCHQ and MI5. You're a very popular man."

The door opened and a man wearing a grey suit entered. He was an older man—about thirty—with thick stubble, his suit crumpled as if he had been sleeping in it. He flashed his ID at the other man.

The black-suited man said, "You guys don't hang around. I didn't expect you for another half hour."

Looking at Taylor, the grey-suited man said, "I was in the area. So, this is Bruce Taylor? Has he said anything?"

"No. I was told not to question him until you got here."

"Good. I've got some paperwork for you to sign."

The grey-suited man took out a sheet of paper and laid it flat on the table.

"They're standard forms to say you've handed him over to us. If you just read this section and sign."

The black-suited man squinted.

"Where?"

"Here," the grey-suited man said, pointing at the paper and holding out a pen.

The black-suited man took the pen and leant over. Then, in one swift movement, the grey-suited man grabbed his jacket collar and slammed his head onto the table. It rebounded like a rubber ball. His eyes in separate orbits, the black-suited man fell to the floor, unconscious.

The grey-suited man turned to Taylor.

"We've held back your flight. You'd better get a move on if you're going to catch it."

"Who are you?" Taylor asked.

"You'd better get going. The girl's waiting for you at the gate."

Taylor and Emily took their window seats in the upper deck. Neither spoke, both wrapped up in their thoughts. The seats around them began to fill. Emily stared out of the window, watching the baggage caddy drive away, its empty cages rattling. The ground crew made their final checks. She was still in a mild state of disbelief at how events had unfolded. She had not expected help after they had been taken to the interview room. She had thought that all was lost; her father condemned to years of suffering. She glanced across at Taylor. His eyes were half-closed, his seat reclined, and his head tilted to one side on the headrest. A minute later, he was fast asleep. Emily felt the tension which had built up in her body over the past two days begin to dissipate. Her shoulders slackened, and she too was soon fast asleep.

30

The first of the winter snow had been falling since daybreak. A thick white blanket covered the entire broad landscape. On the banks of the river, a herd of deer drank from the ice-cold waters. Two stags were locking horns, their thick breathes pooling around their sweaty bodies, whilst other deer poked and prodded hooves and snouts in the brush, chewing on vegetation.

The air was crisp and fresh. Carl Brenner, standing on the dacha's wooden porch, his arms resting on the handrail, holding a hot mug of *sbiten,* stared out at the perfect white snow covering the countryside. The simple beauty of nature was in stark contrast to the urban sprawl that surrounded Stonebridge.

He thought back at his time there with ambivalence. He was not a man who regretted his actions. As far as he was concerned, a man was not a free agent. Surround a man with decadence and debauchery, and the outcome was inevitable. He had a propensity to the baser desires and had always found that trying to suppress them only made them stronger. And so, he yielded.

However, that life had been taken from him when he had fled the country. The stately Jacobean mansion that was Stonebridge was now no more than a fond memory.

He blinked as the sun peeked out from behind the distant mountain range. It was a magnificent view; trees and rolling hills surrounded the dacha. There were still a few patches of green visible. In a few hours, they would all be covered. He turned when he heard a loud knock on the door. Taking a sip from his mug, he went back inside. Opening the front door, he was met by the familiar old face of one of his two permanent minders, Vladimir.

Vladimir was a stocky man, a veteran of Afghanistan. He had deep-set eyes and a fixed, gruff expression on a square face that looked like it had been permanently frozen by the frigid Caucasus winds. He wore a white *ushanka* and thick khaki *telogreika,* which was now covered in a dusting of snow, a packet of cigarettes protruding from the front pocket, and an AK-47 slung over his shoulder. He stamped his heavy boots on the ground, clumps of snow falling off them.

Neither Vladimir nor Alexei, the other minder, were in good shape, both had overhanging bellies, and Alexei was prone to asthmatic attacks. They were more of a token presence.

"Everything OK?" Vladimir asked.

"Fine," Brenner said.

Vladimir was too set in his ways to learn more than a few stock phrases of English. He was also distrustful of any Russian who could fluently speak the language of the enemy. Brenner had made no effort to learn Russian. When he first arrived, he had looked at a beginner's textbook, but the prospect of learning the Cyrillic alphabet was too daunting.

This was a routine check-up, one of four during the day.

"Where's Alexei?" Brenner asked.

"Get food."

"OK. I'm having lunch. Do you want to join me?"

It was a question Brenner always asked, more out of politeness than any desire to actually have lunch with the soldier. As usual, Vladimir declined. Brenner closed the door and went back into the living area. The old soldier lit a cigarette and plodded away through the snow.

For the first month after he escaped from Stonebridge, Brenner had lived in Moscow and had been interviewed by FSB every day. They took copious notes regarding his time in the UK and the names of people he had met. Even though Moscow was a bustling city, Brenner had felt very alone. FSB had supplied him with girls, and he had attended various parties, but he soon tired of them.

It was suggested that he take time off to reflect. It was made clear that the fatherland was grateful for his cooperation. The dacha was in a secluded location and would give him the opportunity to clear his mind. The nearest town was over a hundred miles away, and with the heavy snow to come, this place would soon only be accessible with a snowmobile.

Although Vladimir and Alexei were officially his bodyguards, he doubted his life was in any danger. He had told the Russians everything he knew, and MI5 was not in the business of revenge. They would know that killing him now would make no difference and would only cause a political storm.

Brenner did not miss his past dissolute life but knew he would rather live one day as a free man than a thousand stranded out here. He had taken to reading and had discovered the Tao. Although he had never been a religious man, he found comfort in the wider view of existence it propounded.

He went into the dining room and took his meal of fish and potatoes from the oven. Uncorking a bottle of red wine, he poured himself a glass. After a satisfying lunch, he sat down on the sofa, picked up the book he had started the day before, an introductory guide to Taoism, and began reading from where he had left off.

However, his thoughts soon turned to his last day in Moscow when he had managed to slip away from his minders for a few minutes and find a payphone from where he had called his old number at Stonebridge. Had anyone at GCHQ intercepted the call? Was anyone even living in Stonebridge now? Maybe the mansion was vacant, and there was a light flashing on an answerphone because no one had checked it. Did they even care about what he had said in his message? Time had passed, and maybe it was no longer of any value.

He sighed and turned back to his book. Soon, his eyelids became heavy, and he dozed off.

31

Pritchard slowly lowered the phone and placed it back in its cradle. He stared at Barnes, who was leaning against the office door and said, "They both made it onto the flight."

Barnes's body stiffened.

"What?" he said, gasping.

"The police took them to two separate interview rooms for questioning—standard procedure. Someone overpowered both of the officers."

"Someone? You mean one of us!"

"There aren't many people who can pull off something like that."

"You're thinking of Charters or Anderson."

"Or both."

"The conspiracy."

This time there was no hint of sarcasm in Barnes's words.

Pritchard said, "They're the only two people who know about Taylor and the girl."

"Anderson. I would never have thought he had it in him."

"Don't be fooled by the lumbering exterior. It's all a front. He's a lot smarter than he lets on."

"But why help the Chinese? Do you think they've got something on him?"

"I don't know. We'll find out soon enough. Have you got eyes on him?"

"Yes."

Barnes took out his phone and punched out a number.

"Hammond," he said. "I'm putting you on speaker. What've you got?"

Hammond said, "Last night—eight o'clock—Charters visited Anne Richmond. He left at nine, and she left thirty minutes later. She'd packed a small luggage bag."

Barnes said, "Did you follow her?"

"No, you told me to follow Charters."

Annoyed, Barnes said, "You should have called to ask for instructions."

Hammond said nothing.

"What did he do after he left?" Pritchard said.

"Charters? He went straight home."

Barnes shot Pritchard a nervous glance and said, "You don't know where Richmond went?"

"No. Do you want me to go inside the flat?"

"Where are you now?" Pritchard asked.

"Thames house. Charters is in a meeting."

"Forget Charters!" Pritchard said. "Find out where Richmond went."

"Yes, sir."

Barnes hung up.

"Charters is up to something," Pritchard said. "It's always been him. All those risky ops he dreamt up in the past. It all makes sense now. He wanted them to fail, and the officers eliminated.

"And it explains why he's been so relaxed about Taylor's reappearance. He wanted us to play it slow and not send a team in. It gave him a chance to get him out."

"He sent the girl in?"

"Yes."

"And Anderson?"

Pritchard glared at Barnes and said, "I'm not sure. Charters could be playing him too—using him as a decoy."

Barnes shook his head and said, "I can't believe it. It's just too fantastic. The head of GCHQ, a Chinese mole."

"Have you got another explanation?"

"No. What do we do? Expose him? We haven't got any concrete evidence."

Pritchard got up and said, "We have to tread carefully. We may be able to use this to our advantage, but we should wait until we hear back from Hammond. Charters is taking a big risk. Why?"

32

The wooden barn was over ten feet high and had a slanted roof. Anne navigated her way down the small hill and pulled up outside, parking her car behind a wood chipper. She was relieved that she had finally reached her destination; the drive had been a treacherous one, and although the car's wheels had been fitted with snow chains, there had been several occasions when she had lost control and almost skidded off the road.

Her plane had landed at Domodedovo International Airport late that evening, the runway lights twinkling in the fading twilight. She had managed only a few hours of broken sleep on the flight. Her thoughts kept returning to the plans Charters had laid out in her flat. She would, he explained, take a flight to Volgograd. From there, she would meet up with her first contact, a fisherman who would supply her with a car and provisions for the two-hundred-mile drive to the secluded dacha. After acquiring the necessary information from Brenner, the two of them were to head to the border with Kazakhstan, where another contact would make arrangements to get them back home.

Sitting at her window seat, Anne fell deep into thought when the plane began to circle Samara Oblast, located in the basin of the Volga River. To the north, the vast expanse of coniferous and broadleaved woods. Her mind was focused on the river. It was over two thousand miles long, but she could not help thinking that she was looking down at the very spot where her husband's body had been found.

Her contact in Volgograd knew nothing of her true identity. He was a squat man of indeterminate age with a jaundiced complexion, prominent cheekbones, epicanthic folds about the eyes, and straight black hair. During the hour she spent in his wood-framed shack, he kept his family hidden from her, confined to a bedroom. On the one occasion that she had walked past the room, a small child had peered out. Anne saw a young, frightened-looking woman inside the bedroom—the man's daughter or possibly even his wife—sitting on an animal skin rug by an open hearth, a baby cradled in her arms. The man barked a command, and the child abruptly closed the door.

The shack had an overpowering stench of fish—many of which were hung from hooks in the main room that doubled up as a smokehouse.

The man did not speak Russian, and his English consisted of two words: yes and no. Anne had to use simple gestures such as pointing at her watch and spooning imaginary food into her mouth when clarifying details of journey time and provisions he had to pack in the car for her.

It was a relief when she was ready to leave, a relief to be free from the keen eyes of the fisherman, which were continually straying to catch a furtive glance at her watch and clothes. His eyes lit up when it was time to be paid, and he made a point of emphasising that he had filled up the tank, gesturing with an imaginary jerry can. Anne paid him an additional two thousand roubles, which seemed to satisfy him.

The car was old, pitted with rust, and the brake pedal felt spongy, but Anne would have taken a horse and cart if that had been all the fisherman had. She just wanted to get out of his oppressive presence.

There was never a moment she could relax on the drive. The rippled tarmac and bumps in the highway—a consequence of sweltering summers and sub-zero winters—ensured that driving demanded her full attention. She saw only two cars on her journey, both heading in the opposite direction.

When she finally made it to the hamlet, she headed straight to the barn. Sacks of grain were stacked up against the walls, straw laid down over the wooden floor. She decided to keep the car outside; she did not expect to be here long.

She surveyed the surrounding area. The dacha was about eight hundred metres from the hamlet. Plumes of smoke rose from the small wooden dwellings. An elderly woman wrapped in a thick shawl trudged back from a well, a pail of water held in her calloused hands.

The rear door of the dacha was ajar. Anne crept forward and then broke into a sprint. As she leapt onto the porch, her feet skidded on a thin layer of loose snow. She held her breath and managed to keep upright. She took out her gun and slowly opened the door, which creaked as she pushed it back.

The room was warm, a stove burning in the corner. She looked at the man asleep on the sofa, a paperback on the floor by his feet. The man's eyes flickered open. For a moment, the two of them stared at each other.

"You got my message?" Brenner said.

"We got it."

Anne glanced around.

"It's safe to talk?" she asked.

"Yes. Even if the place is bugged, they wouldn't have someone listening now. It's not as if I'm expected to have visitors."

Brenner hauled himself to his feet.

"You're here to get me out?"

"Yes. Provided you have what we want."

"I've got it. Are you from MI5?"

"GCHQ."

"Oh, I don't suppose it matters."

"Well, where is it?"

"I don't have it on me. If I did, I'd be dead. You can't hide things like that from them. It's in a safe place."

Brenner went over to Anne.

"How did you get here?"

"Car."

Brenner looked out of the window and said, "We'd better get a move on. The snow's starting to get heavy."

"Not without the information."

Brenner smiled.

"You're not a trusting lot, are you? All right."

He picked up the book on the floor, took it over to a desk, pressed back the cover and began writing. He went back to Anne and handed it to her.

"You'll find everything here," he said.

Anne glanced at the address he had written down.

Brenner added, "You don't know what it is, do you?"

Anne considered.

"You're going to have to trust me," Brenner said.

"OK. Let's go. The car's behind the barn."

Glancing at his watch, Brenner said, "Wait. I've got two minders. One of them's due to make a routine check about now."

"Then, what are we waiting for? Let's move."

"No. They check up every four hours, and then they go back to their quarters. It's just a quick check; Vladimir doesn't even come inside. He should be here in a few minutes. After he leaves, we'll have a good four-hour start on them."

Anne took a moment to consider, glancing out at the falling snow. Every minute spent waiting was more time for the roads to become impassable.

"OK," she agreed uneasily.

"Would you like a smoke while you wait?"

"No."

Brenner took a packet from the table.

"I've been pretty much cut off from the world for three years. I know there was a big fuss when I got out. Do they still call me a traitor back home?"

"Does it matter?" Anne asked, sitting down.

"I don't know why—at first, it didn't—but it does now."

"So, you would've done things differently if you had the chance again."

"I can't change what's happened, but if I do the right thing now … if I could—"

There was a loud bang on the door. Anne and Brenner exchanged an uneasy glance.

"Wait on the porch," Brenner whispered.

Anne slipped out of the back door. Brenner swallowed and went over and opened the front door.

"Everything OK?" Vladimir said.

"Fine."

The two men stood for a moment, not saying anything.

Closing the door, Brenner said, "I'm a bit tired. I think I'll take a nap."

Vladimir pushed out his hand and held the door open.

Scrutinising Brenner, he said, "You not ask me to have drink?"

"Oh, I didn't think you wanted one. W-would you like one?"

"Yes."

The column of Brenner's neck constricted. He forced a smile.

"Come in. It must be cold out there."

Vladimir grunted and stepped inside. His small, beady eyes darted about the room.

Anne, who had been watching through a half-open door, pulled her head back. He knows, she thought. She looked across at the barn. The only footsteps in the snow were the ones she had left when she had run to the dacha. None were leading to it. He knows. But how?

Vladimir walked around the room.

"That drink," Brenner said, trying to keep his voice level. "Vodka?"

"*Sbiten*. I smoke?"

"Please, go ahead."

A sudden deluge of snow fell. How much longer? Anne thought. The car was old and had taken several attempts to start when she had left Volgograd. I should just kill him, she thought. But there is the possibility that he suspects nothing. She didn't want to kill unless she had no choice. She hoped that Brenner wouldn't fold like Woodstein.

Brenner came back into the living area with a mug of *sbiten*. His hand shaking, he handed it to Vladimir, who had made himself comfortable on the sofa, his AK-47 on the armrest.

"You cold?" Vladimir asked.

"A bit. I suppose you're used to it?"

Vladimir grunted and took a sip of his drink. He put the mug down and picked up the paperback on the table.

He studied the Chinese calligraphy on the cover.

"You read this?" he asked.

"It's in English. It's a book about Taoism. That's a Chinese philosophy."

Vladimir fanned out the pages. He turned back to the inside cover.

Showing Brenner the scribbled address, he said, "What this?"

"I make notes when I read."

"This address? No?"

"No, just a note."

A shadow passed over the veteran's face.

Getting to his feet, he said, "I take it."

"Is that necessary?" Brenner asked, trying to keep his voice steady.

Vladimir said nothing and picked up his rifle.

"You haven't finished your *sbiten*," Brenner said.

"I go."

In the corner of his eye, Vladimir saw Anne's shadow against the wall. He spun around and raised his rifle. Realising what was happening, Brenner threw himself on the veteran, who thrust the butt of his rifle into Brenner's face. Brenner fell to the floor, holding his mouth. Vladimir raised his rifle just as Anne emerged from the doorway. The barrel of her gun lit up with flashes of light as she shot straight at Vladimir's chest. The soldier's body jerked from side to side. He groaned and grabbed his chest, blood seeping out of his wounds. His knees buckled, and he collapsed, dead on the floor.

Anne rushed over to Brenner.

"Are you hurt?" she asked, helping him to his feet.

Brenner rubbed his jaw and looked down at Vladimir.

"No. Let's go."

Anne jumped from the porch into the snow and started to run. Brenner, lagging behind, tried to keep up. The two of them waded through the snow, which was now ankle deep. In the distance could be heard yells. Anne looked across at the hamlet. A small group had gathered, staring and pointing at the dacha. One of them was wearing a khaki *telogreika*, in his hand, a rifle.

"They must have heard the gunshots," Anne yelled.

Brenner, panting, nodded his head. He was only a hundred feet from the car now, each step in the snow sapping his energy. Anne reached the car and slid into the driver's seat. She turned the key, the engine sputtered and then fell silent. She tried again. Again, the engine coughed and choked but refused to catch and fell silent.

"What's wrong?" Brenner asked, trying to catch his breath.

"It must be the cold. I'll try again."

"No, you'll flood the engine."

Brenner looked up at the hill. There was a slight downhill slope before the ascent.

"I can push it," he said. "It might help."

"You're sure?"

A loud crack of another shot rang out. Brenner wiped away the sweat from his face.

"We have to try," he said.

Anne got out and pushed against the car's open door, steering with her free hand, while Brenner pushed from the rear. When the car reached the top of the slope, Anne leapt in. Brenner took a deep breath and pushed with all his strength. The car rolled forward and immediately picked up speed down the gentle slope. Anne, her face rigid with fear and hope, turned the key. The engine sputtered and, this time, did not die. Wild relief leapt through her. She pressed down on the brake, slowed the car, and waited for Brenner to catch up.

"Get in," she said, her voice rising hysterically.

She watched Brenner in the wing mirror as he made laboured progress through the snow. He paused to catch his breath, bent double, his hand on his knees. Two shots rang out, and he was propelled forward, stumbling before he fell in a heap in the snow. Anne leapt out of the car and ran over to him. Brenner lay on his side, a red patch of blood growing in the snow. Anne crouched beside him. He looked up at her, a watery smile on his face. He opened his mouth as if to speak, but his head fell limp into the snow. Anne's eyes sparkled with tears.

She got up. Two more shots rang out, sending up puffs of snow a few feet from where she stood. The man wearing the *telogreika* had his rifle aimed at her, peering intently into the viewfinder. Anne threw herself into the snow as more shots rang out. She crawled back to the car, got in and slammed shut the door. She stood on the throttle, and the tyres spun wildly as they fought for traction, the snow chains biting into the ground. The car lurched forward and slowly began to ascend the hill.

Progress was slow in the snow. But after an hour of driving, Anne was sure she had no pursuers. They had, she knew, taken the logical step of radioing ahead to the next town. It would be insane to drive in these conditions—let alone pursue anyone. She would have to steer clear of the next town and make it straight to the border, but that would mean adding another hundred miles to her journey. She glanced down at the petrol gauge; she still had half a tank. She turned the heating up, but it had little effect. She glanced at the clock on the dashboard. Her contact on the border had been told to expect her in three hours. She doubted she would make it in time.

She gripped the wheel as the car skidded from side to side. All her concentration was needed to keep the car on the road, and she did not have time to think about Brenner. She had made it out, and she had the information Charters wanted. The op was a success.

A wave of euphoria washed over her. She could think back about the bullets flying past her and the escape from the dacha with a feeling of exhilaration. She had made it out. She had never felt so alive.

She steered towards a grove of trees that ran along a ravine. The snow was not as thick there, and she could still see the faint black of a tarmac road. She turned the wheel and slowly navigated over to the road. She felt she had more control of the car and increased her speed.

Suddenly, she lost the rear end. She corrected with a sharp turn of the wheel, but it was too late. The car skidded across the ice, and then she felt the ground give way beneath her. Her senses became heightened, and everything seemed to be happening in slow motion. The earth rose above her, and the sky turned black. She braced herself.

A hard, blinding thud on the back of her head was the last thing she remembered before being knocked unconscious.

33

Taylor and Emily stood under the archway of Beijing Capital International Airport. In the distance, skyscrapers disappeared into the thick morning smog that hung heavy in the air. The pale-yellow disc of the sun hung low in the sky. Beneath it, the asymmetrical arch of the China Central TV Headquarters glinted in the hazy sunlight.

Emily signalled to one of the two-tone orange-and-blue taxis parked in the taxi rank. The driver, who had been sitting at the wheel reading a newspaper, folded it and started up the engine.

"The Forbidden City," Emily said.

Emily and Taylor got in, and the taxi drove off. It was a quiet afternoon by Beijing standards, the traffic flowing freely on the six-lane road. Soon, the airport's landscaped surroundings were lost from view as they approached the urban sprawl of the city.

A loud boom reverberated. Emily looked out of the window as a large residential block collapsed, its walls falling in on themselves, disappearing into a mushroom cloud of smoke and debris that reached up high into the hazy sky. A small knot of former residents, wearing ragged clothes, looked on, their dirty, unwashed faces glum and resigned. Beside them, donkeys were tethered to rickety carts laden with a lifetime of belongings: cheap rugs, wooden furniture and bundles of clothes tied up with string.

Emily was reminded of the old Chinese saying: if the old doesn't go, the new won't come. Nowhere was that truer than here in Beijing. She had been out of the country for just over a year, and in that time, hundreds of new buildings had been constructed with ruthless efficiency. Old residential blocks were razed, and new construction sites were taking their place. A layer of white soot had settled on the road. Emily pulled up the window. Change was indeed the only constant in a city like Beijing.

The taxi entered Chang'an Avenue. The traffic was heavy, and the taxi slowed to a crawl and then a halt at the traffic lights. Through the fine mist of exhaust fumes, Emily could see the monolithic Great Hall of the People. The red flags in front of it hung limp on masts.

She had been inside once during a school trip. As impressive as the façade was, the interior was even more breathtaking. Her class had been led through the magnificent rooms named after the twenty-nine Chinese provinces of the universe, and then they went into the auditorium itself. It was grand and majestic, yet soulless.

Her teacher had informed the pupils, in a well-rehearsed spiel, that the people are the masters of the country. It was to emphasise this point that the architect had designed such a splendid building.

She said, "Do not be fooled by the illusion of Western democracy."

She explained how Western democracy was a deception that simply handed power over to a small clique of privileged individuals. Here in the vast auditorium, all the people of the republic had a voice. Millions of people were disenfranchised and bitter around the world, even though they lived in so-called democracies. In reality, they were merely submitting themselves to the power of a great Leviathan and living out their lives in subjugation. That would never happen here in the motherland.

At the time, she had been too young to understand what her teacher espoused. But now, she remembered the words with a feeling of bitterness. Across from the Great Hall was Tiananmen Square. The flash of a camera caught her attention. The square was filled with tourists. A young man with a backpack adorned with the Stars and Stripes ambled amongst the hordes.

More tourists funnelled through the five archways of the vermillion platform on which Tiananmen Tower stood, a portrait of Mao hanging over the central archway. When built in the seventeenth century, the archway was reserved for use only by the emperors. Now, it was for the masses.

Like herself, many of the tourists had not even been born during the failed uprising of 1989. But for her, the square would forever be linked to the image of a young student who would not yield in front of the tanks as they rolled through the streets, the black cloud of martial law descending upon the city. The brutal crackdown which ensued resulted in hundreds if not thousands of deaths.

Emily glanced across at Taylor. He turned to her and smiled, reaching out to hold her hand. She felt a pang in her heart. The price for her father's freedom was a high one.

"Is anything the matter?" Taylor asked.

Emily shook her head.

"No, I was just thinking."

She glanced at the driver; his unblinking eyes stared back at her in the rearview mirror.

34

Anne's eyes flickered open. By degrees, she regained consciousness. The throbbing of blood in her ears subsided, replaced by the howling wind funnelling through the twisted wreckage of the car. It took a moment for her to remember where she was and what had happened. It was dark, the only light that of the car radio which faintly illuminated the dashboard. She reached up and wiped flakes of snow from her face.

The car was resting at a forty-five-degree angle at the bottom of the ravine. The roof was dented and bent; the shattered windows partially obscured the sky but gave some shelter. Without it, she would have been buried deep in snow. She was lying on her back, the backrest of the seat having collapsed into the rear. A searing pain spread out through her leg when she tried to move it; her femur had snapped in two like a twig, and her foot, trapped beneath the brake pedal, pointed at right angles to her leg.

She tried to pull her leg free and let out a scream. It was wedged between the bent steering column and the crumpled passenger's seat. She took out her satellite phone. The screen was cracked, the battery critically low. She reached over, opened the glove compartment, took out Brenner's book and typed the address he had scribbled on the inside cover. She pressed send and waited for confirmation that the message had been sent, but the screen's light faded, and the phone died.

She threw the phone down. Not angry, not sad, just knowing there was nothing she could do anymore. How often in the past year, she had wanted to die, to be with him—her beloved Sam.

But now, she realised that it was true that people who often wish for death are the ones who fight hardest to keep a hold of life. She had to find a way out.

Even if she did manage to extricate herself, the car was wrecked, and she was over a hundred miles from the nearest town. Without any injury, wading through the thick snow would take a week, at least. With a broken leg and the temperature falling fast, it was impossible.

She wondered how long she would be out here before someone found her body. The barren tundra was vast, and she was probably the only living thing for miles. They wouldn't find her body until the spring when the snow thawed.

She thought about her life. She had done a lot in her twenty-eight years, more than most people who had lived twice as long. All things considered, it had been a good life. It would have made a decent film. A wry smile spread across her lips when she thought of the actors who could play her part.

It hadn't been the kind of life you could openly share with anyone. In many ways, it had been a solitary one, spent working alone on covert ops. All the more reason why she didn't want to die alone out here in the cold night.

She looked far into the distance. A car's headlights flickered through the growing blizzard of snow. She couldn't tell whether it was moving towards or away from her. She rubbed her eyes which were watery from the cold. When she looked again, the light was gone. It didn't make any difference; the road was thirty feet above, and with the wind rising, she would not be heard even if she screamed. She punched the steering wheel— nothing. The horn, too, was broken.

Keep thinking, she thought, her teeth chattering. She was afraid that if she simply gave in and closed her eyes, she would never open them again. She thought of Brenner lying in the snow. What had he wanted to say? Was he sorry for what he had done? Now, he would always be considered a traitor by both sides. It didn't seem fair that a man could be condemned for one mistake in life. No one would ever know that he had tried to do the right thing in the end.

Just meeting him for a few moments had made everything so much more personal. If it hadn't been for this meeting, she would—like many of the public—have considered him in black-and-white terms, not appreciating that he was simply just another flawed human being like everyone else.

She pulled up her collar. Her fingers numb, she thrust her hands deep into her pockets. It will be just like going to sleep. There were worse ways to die. No, she thought. I mustn't give up. If she could get out, she could bury herself in the snow. Using the insulation it provided, she would have a chance—albeit slim—of surviving. Here in the car, death was a certainty.

She tried again to free herself, but still, the pain was too intense, and she had to give up. Brenner's book lay on the seat beside her, its pages fluttering in the wind. She picked it up. Everything would be so much easier if there were a God to believe in, she thought. Yes, everything would have a purpose, then. All the things she had done in her life, even the failures, would have meaning. The more she considered the possibility of a God watching over her, the more the thought comforted her, and she did not feel so alone.

35

DCI Hall put down the desk phone and looked at the name she had just scribbled on her notepad: Lyle Anderson, Head of A Branch, MI5.

Hall had professional respect towards members of the secret service but was also wary of them. Respect, because she had always entertained a *Girls Own Adventure* fantasy of living outside the law, engaged in dangerous covert ops; wary, because, like most police officers, she was territorial and felt that in recent years the secret service's remit had become all-encompassing.

Early on in her investigation into the Mountview Hospital murders, she had been aware that hidden forces were taking a keen interest in its progress. So, Anderson's request to see her was not entirely unexpected. Had he been the one making enquiries into the fight in the high street which never took place? Was he involved in Taylor and Emily's escape from the airport? Hopefully, she would finally get some answers and move the investigation along.

There was a knock on the door, and she got up.

"Come in."

Anderson entered.

"Pleased to meet you, Mr Anderson."

They shook hands cordially.

Hall said, "I understand you want to talk about the Mountview Hospital murders?"

"Yes."

Hall indicated a chair. Anderson sat down, and Hall took her seat behind her desk.

Anderson said, "I must say that I'm very impressed that you've been able to keep Belakovsky's name out of the papers."

"No problem at all," Hall said casually.

"Really?"

"It's been no problem because Belakovsky isn't dead."

"I don't follow you. Dr Peters' statement ..."

"Peters has never seen Belakovsky in the flesh. The man who was murdered looked a lot like Belakovsky—a lot like him—but it wasn't him. The real Belakovsky is in Moscow."

"And the other two victims?"

"I've no idea who they are. They've come up blank on all our databases. And now, there've been four more murders in London: a middle-aged couple, a postman and a talent agent. Ballistic tests have confirmed that they were all shot using the same gun? I think these murders are related to the ones at the hospital. What do you think?"

"I wouldn't know. Why do you think they're related?"

"We showed Peters photographs of them, and he confirmed that they'd posed as Emily's parents.

"Why have you come here, Mr Anderson? Why are you so interested in this case? Is there something I should know? I know someone's been keeping tabs on the investigation, making enquiries about the fight in the high street—a fight which never took place—and trying to find out what leads we're following up."

"I don't know anything about that."

"Mr Anderson, there is only one law in this country, and it applies to everyone. No one can murder with impunity."

"Have you had any luck finding Taylor and Emily?"

"They're both in Beijing. They were detained at Heathrow yesterday. It seems someone didn't want them to talk, and they escaped. The transport police have got two officers in hospital with concussion."

Anderson frowned, lost in thought. All the pieces were now falling into place in his mind. The realisation of what this all meant weighed down heavy on his mind. He let out a sigh.

"I see," he said.

"Do you? Because I'm still in the dark. Care to enlighten me? We are supposed to be on the same side."

Hall stood looking down from her office window at the street below. Anderson emerged. His chauffeur opened the rear door of his car, and he got in. Hall felt sorry for the old man. There was such a palpable look of resignation in his eyes when she had told him that Taylor and Emily had received help to escape. No, he wasn't bluffing, she thought. He didn't know anything about the case. Whatever games of subterfuge and deception these agencies played extended even to their own staff.

People had been killed and lives ruined. Most notably, Peters's. He was now a shell of his former self. He had been a wreck when she had interviewed him at the hospital, but now he had been signed off indefinitely with stress. When she had visited him at home to update him on the progress of the case and to tell him that an imposter and not Belakovsky had been murdered, she had been shocked by his dishevelled appearance. He was listless and had taken to drinking. He no longer cared about his career and was content to slip into oblivion.

Anderson gave every impression of being a tired old man. He had seemingly aged before her eyes, his body sagging with every second. Hall's *Girls Own Adventure* fantasy had lost its lustre; she was glad that she was not a part of this shadowy world.

Anderson was tired of the whole spying game. He stared out of the window of his car as it ground to a halt at the traffic lights. Questions kept plaguing his thoughts—questions which inextricably led to one conclusion.

From the very beginning, Charters could have moved to have had Taylor extracted from the hospital—it would have been a routine thing to arrange—but he hadn't. He had given Pritchard a free hand to act how he chose, and he had not put any pressure on him since the debacle of Taylor's escape. It was out of character for Charters to let things get this out of control.

Innocent people were being murdered, and Taylor and Emily had escaped to China. The revelation that someone had helped them get on the flight had settled matters in Anderson's mind. This was the first he had heard of this. Only Charters had the authority to pull resources together at such short notice without going through channels.

Anderson couldn't act unilaterally even if he was certain that Charters was a mole. There were procedures in place for such scenarios. How many others would there be? How many other friends, old friends, were involved? They would all have to be unmasked. It would be horrible to see them exposed as traitors.

And what had motivated Charters? Not ideology, of that, Anderson was sure. Charters wasn't political in any sense. Money? Had he sold himself into some Faustian pact with the Chinese for money? That, too, made no sense. Charters was a well-paid man who would get a generous pension when he retired.

Whatever Charters motivation, Anderson couldn't stand by and let Pritchard and others be eliminated. That was what all this was about: elimination. He didn't have any real liking for

Pritchard. How could anyone? The man was so cold and distant, but he couldn't condemn him out of some misplaced loyalty to an old friend.

36

Emily and Taylor stepped into the outer courtyard of the Forbidden City. Tourists were milling about, taking photographs, eating and enjoying the view of the three large palaces.

Emily didn't expect to see secret service agents conspicuously standing around, wearing black suits and shades. They would be more covert, not positioned too close but far enough away to be able to survey the whole square and see if she made contact with anyone. Her outburst in the embassy with Han had been a mistake. It was clear that they did not fully trust her and were holding back from making contact.

She glanced around but saw no one that she suspected of being an agent. They would probably be waiting inside the Palace Museum, where they would have a greater degree of control. Out here, if things went wrong, there were too many people, too many variables to take into account.

"What do we do now?" Taylor said.

"We walk around like all the other tourists until they decide to make contact."

They traversed the square, entered the Palace Museum and admired the vases and paintings on display. It was difficult not to be in awe of such a building. Every civilisation, Emily thought, had moments of true enlightenment, and there was no better example than the Forbidden City.

She recognised one of the paintings of a lotus flower as the original of one she had seen in the embassy. She paused to look at it and thought back to Han sitting in the meeting room and the hidden eyes that watched her from the concealed camera in the statue of Mao.

Reflexively, she turned and appraised the security guard standing at the door. He stared fixedly back at her. An elderly man with a walking stick stole a furtive glance in her direction. Everyone, or so it seemed to her, was staring at them.

They moved on to the Halls of Harmony and were soon standing amongst a group of tourists in front of the Dragon Throne, the dragon motifs lining the ramp by which the emperor had once ascended to his seat of power.

Emily glanced at her watch. It had been over thirty minutes since they had arrived, and still no contact. She looked across at Taylor, who was idly glancing around.

"Excuse me, madam."

Emily and Taylor turned around.

A small man wearing a western suit gave a slight bow.

"My name is Zhang Wei. If you would accompany me, please."

Taylor and Emily fell in behind Wei as he led them out of the main hall down a corridor and into a side room. Two soldiers, wearing full Chinese army uniforms, were sitting in the corner. They got to their feet and pointed their rifles at Taylor.

Wei turned to Emily and said, "You have done well. You did everything we asked of you."

Life left Taylor's body. He stared at Emily.

"My father?" she said.

"He is waiting for you in a house on the Third Ring Road. There is a car waiting outside for you. We honour our agreements. He has not been harmed. You are free to leave."

Emily turned to Taylor, his face ashen, and said, "I'm sorry. I had no choice."

Taylor remained silent. Emily turned away, her eyes filling with tears. Taylor grabbed her by the arm.

"That's it? Sorry. That's all you've got to say?"

"I did it for my father. I didn't want it to end like this. They gave me no choice."

"There never was an 'us', was there?"

Emily shook her head.

"No."

"Was any of it true?"

"Some of it. I told you what you needed to know—wanted to hear."

She pulled her arm free from his and left the room.

Taylor turned to Wei, who had stood patiently, waiting for the scene to end.

Emily closed the door and pressed her back against it. A feeling of relief swept through her. It was over. The nightmare was finally over.

From inside the room, she heard a thud and then a groan. She tore herself away from the door and quickly walked down the corridor. Don't think about it, she thought. It's done. There's no going back, now. She walked toward the double doors that led out into the main hall but stopped when she reached them. If she walked through these doors, she could return to her life with her father. Her father was free; she had got what she wanted. She had known from the moment that she had left the embassy that this was how it would end.

Taylor was not an innocent party. He was a killer who had assassinated countless people. Why should she show him mercy when he had shown none to those he had eliminated?

But the image of Taylor's face as realisation of her duplicity dawned on him loomed up before her, and her arguments seemed lame. It was the only way, she told herself. It may not have been the good thing to do, but it was the right thing.

Yet, she had feelings for him now. He was not the man he had been. She was condemning him for things he did not even remember doing. Her mind struggled for a clear resolution. Could she let him die? Could one life be exchanged for another? His for her father's. No, she thought. There must be another way.

She turned around, marched back to the room and, pressing her ear against the door, heard several thuds and groans. What am I doing, she thought? They're armed soldiers in there. I wouldn't have a chance against them.

However, Wei reminded her of Han. He was too sure of himself and considered the job done and dusted, and the two soldiers came across as complacent because they had total faith in their superior's judgement.

Should she burst in and attack them or knock on the door and use subterfuge to get close to one of the soldiers and grab his rifle. They were young, probably not very experienced and would not be expecting anything. No, she decided. She would have to act decisively and with intent. Taylor was in a foreign country, alone. They would not expect him to have any help.

Taking a deep breath, she threw open the door and stormed in. Taylor was lying on the floor, the two soldiers standing over him. Wei was sitting in a chair, his hands on his lap. Startled, he looked up at Emily, an expression of puzzlement on his face.

Emily ran up to him, and with a fast, vicious movement, punched him in the throat. He gasped, grabbed his neck and fell off the chair, his body convulsing. The two soldiers stared in disbelief. They fumbled with their rifles, but Emily had already rushed up to them. Again, she delivered a devastating blow to the throat of one soldier and then kicked the other between the legs. Both men fell to the floor, writhing about in agony.

Wei rolled onto his back, his face turning blue, his breathing laboured. He reached into his pocket and pulled out a gun. Emily rushed over and kicked it out of his hand. As she did so, the gun discharged into Wei's face, killing him instantly.

Emily walked over to Taylor, who was slowly regaining consciousness.

"Bruce," she said, taking him by the arm and helping him up.

There was blood trickling from a gash on Taylor's temple, and blood drummed in his ears. Emily's voice was muffled and unintelligible. Slowly, he opened his eyes and saw a blur of colours; everything around him looked vague and insubstantial.

"I'm not Bruce Taylor. My name's John Hunter."

37

Three years earlier

It was a balmy Sunday evening in Hamburg. Hunter sat in the back seat of his car parked across from the four-storey townhouse at the corner of the cobbled street, his gaze never straying from its entrance. He pulled down his sleeve; his illuminated watch dial displayed seven o'clock.

He sat motionless, lurking in the shadows, as the last of the late shoppers browsed storefronts and meandered casually along the street.

An hour elapsed, and the sun descended behind the high buildings, gilding their roofs. The last of the shops closed, and soon the street was deserted. As darkness fell, the lights in the flats above the shops were, one by one, switched on. The street was illuminated with faint yellow lozenges of light shining through stained windows.

A shopkeeper wheeled out a bin and left it on the pavement. Hunter heard the raucous laughter of a group of men making their way to a local bar at the far end of the street.

He heard the soft purr of the approaching moped. Soon the bright beam of its headlights blinded him as it came over the brow of the hill and pulled up outside the townhouse. The rider and pillion, both wearing full-face helmets, dismounted. The rider was a big, broad-shouldered man. Hunter could not make out with certainty if the pillion was a woman or a small man. They stood for a moment, the rider glancing up and down at the cars parked on both sides of the street.

Hunter reached for his gun. There was a temptation to finish the job here and eliminate both the rider and pillion. He reached over for the door handle and then immediately pulled back. In the tail of his eye, he had seen a car pull up at the rear of the townhouse. A small figure wearing a hoodie got out and went in the back door. Once again, Hunter was unsure as to whether it was a man or woman.

A decoy, he realised. The rider and pillion went inside. Hunter waited for a full ten minutes before the pillion re-emerged. However, now, the pillion's jacket didn't fit as snugly as before, and his leather trousers were pulled up a tad higher than they had been, exposing red socks as he got on the moped. He started up the engine and, after performing a U-turn, drove away back up the hill.

Hunter waited another five minutes until he was satisfied the switch had been completed. He got out of the car and went into the building.

The townhouse had been divided into flats. At its centre was a spiral staircase wrapped around a lift. Hunter ascended the stairs, and as he approached the third-floor landing, he peered up through the bannister and saw the shadow of a man standing guard outside a flat. He took out his gun, fitted with a silencer, and, after a moment to compose himself, sprinted up the remaining steps.

"*Halt!*" the leather-clad moped rider said, holding out a hand.

He wore dark glasses, and his face, which had been an expressionless granite mask, registered a surge of frantic emotion. He reached for the bulge in his jacket pocket, but Hunter was too quick and shot him between the eyes at point-blank range, catching his lifeless body and slowly lowering it down onto the floor.

Hunter opened the door to the flat. A naked woman was sprawled on a rug in front of an unlit fireplace, her torso slicked with sweat. Her breast violently heaved up and down, her eyes half-open. She turned to see who had entered. Her face contorted, and she screamed when she saw the body of the guard slumped outside. Hunter unleashed a quick burst of fire at her chest. Blood oozed out of wounds forming streaks across her sweaty skin.

The kitchen door opened, and a naked man emerged, holding a champagne glass in each hand. He gaped foolishly at Hunter before dropping the glasses, rushing back inside the kitchen and slamming shut the door. Hunter ran over and kicked open the door. A knife flew past his head. The man was fumbling in the dish rack, searching for another weapon. Hunter shot him once in the chest. The man clasped his chest and fell to his knees. Hunter walked up to him, grabbed him by the hair and pulled back his head. He thrust the nozzle of the silencer into the man's mouth and pulled the trigger. The bullet punched through the back of the man's skull, splattering blood and brain tissue on the wall. The man's arms fell limp at his side. Hunter released his grip and let the man fall face down onto the floor.

Back out in the street, Hunter headed straight for his car. No emotions passed through his mind; it had been just another successful op. He knew nothing about the man he had killed.

He stopped in the middle of the street. In the corner of his eye, he caught the flash of something metallic. He looked across at a small black car parked in the corner and immediately saw the long telephoto lens propped up on the steering wheel. He sprinted over to it. The paparazzo at the wheel started the engine and frantically turned the steering wheel. Hunter let out a silent burst of fire, and the windscreen instantly transformed into an opaque mass of fractured glass. The car gunned forward, straight at Hunter and hit him, throwing him off his feet and sending him rolling over the bonnet before landing on the cobblestones. The car came to an abrupt halt.

Hunter shook his head and got to his feet. He reached up and touched his forehead. When he looked at his hand, he saw that it was smeared with blood. He staggered back to the car and pulled open the driver's door. Inside, the paparazzo, a young man, was slumped in his seat. There was blood splattered everywhere.

"Bitte töte mich nicht. Ich habe eine Frau und Sohn!"

Hunter looked across at the camera lying on the seat and then back at the paparazzo before shooting him between the eyes.

"You did everything we asked of you," Charters said.

He looked down at Hunter, who sat bolt upright, his hands clenching tight the armrests on his chair.

They were in a small briefing room. Other than the chair in which Hunter sat, the only other furniture was a low metal desk behind which Dr Henley stood, leafing through papers on a clipboard.

Hunter looked from Charters to Henley and said, "I killed innocent people."

"No," Charters said, shaking his head. "Everyone we sent you to eliminate was an enemy of the state. The man you killed last night was a TV producer running a drug route from Columbia into London via Hamburg.

"I killed a photographer in a car!"

"Oh, him," Charters said, turning to Henley, who had come up beside him. "A paparazzi—collateral damage."

Hunter stared down at the floor.

"We're losing him," Henley said. "He'll sink further and further into the abyss."

"Can't you …" Charters groped in his mind for the word. "Fix him?"

Henley shook his head.

"He took a big hit from the car. The electrodes have been misaligned. They're firing up a different part of the brain now. The part responsible for emotions."

"You mean remorse, guilt."

"Yes."

"Then realign them."

"It doesn't work that way. He's feeling guilt for what he's done. Whatever we do now will not change that. The only way to get rid of those thoughts would be to wipe the associated memories."

Anticipating Charters follow-up question, Henley added, "That's not something we know how to do. We're not advanced enough to wipe selective memories. However, there is the possibility that we could modify the memory of last night. But that carries risks."

"Explain."

"Memories are not stored in your brain like photographs or films. When we remember, we reconstruct our memories each time. If you want to recall things accurately, you can't have any outside distractions. If you do, memories can become distorted. This is how false memories can be implanted, and they can be indistinguishable from the real ones.

"For example, imagine a person remembers going to the cinema. It's a vague memory, and he's not sure about all the details. It's possible to suggest to him that it had been raining even though it hadn't. When he recalls that event on a future occasion, he may well remember it as having been raining on that day."

"This wasn't a trip to a cinema. He shot a paparazzi."

"That's why it would be difficult. We would have to find a whole new scenario for why he was in Hamburg in the first place."

"Not just Hamburg. He's done over twenty ops. We could just erase everything."

"That wouldn't be ethical."

"Ethical? Nothing about this programme is ethical."

"But there are degrees. We shouldn't …"

Hunter looked up at the two men. He heard what they were saying, but only some of it made sense. All he could think about was the woman and child who had been left fatherless because of what he had done.

"I want to forget," he said.

Charters and Henley stopped talking and turned to him.

"I want to forget *everything*," Hunter said.

"He's in no fit state to make such a decision," Henley said.

Without hesitation, Hunter said, "It's what I want—to forget."

"You're sure you want to do this?" Charters said. "You know what it would mean?"

"Yes," Hunter said, nodding.

Charters turned to Henley and said, "You can do it?"

"Yes, Henley said. "But I can't guarantee anything. If it does work, you'll be a different person."

"A better person?" Hunter said. "The pain will go?"

"Yes," Henley said. "If it works, there'll be no more pain."

38

Emily released her grip on Hunter's arm and took a step back.

"Who are you?" Hunter said.

Emily glanced at the soldiers rolling about on the floor and then at Wei with his face obliterated by the gunshot.

"We can't talk here," she said grimly.

They half-ran out of the room and down the corridor and were soon outside. Tiananmen Square was still bustling with tourists. Breaking into a brisk run, the two of them quickly ascended the steps that led back out onto Chang'an Avenue.

A white Haval H6 was parked conspicuously, blocking a lane of traffic. The driver, a slim man wearing a sharp black suit, stood beside it. When the occasional car honked its horn, he would turn and give a withering stare at the driver, who would then meekly cower behind the wheel and navigate around the Haval.

"He's waiting for you," Hunter said.

The two of them parted. Emily approached the driver, and he opened the door for her. Hunter's rapid punch in the back of his head rendered him immediately unconscious. Emily caught him before he fell to the ground. The two of them carried him to the side of the road. Pedestrians walked quickly past, not wanting to get involved.

Hunter and Emily got in the car. Emily stabbed a button on the dashboard. The blue lights on the front grill flashed, and a siren wailed. A path cleared before them. Emily slammed her foot down on the throttle, and the car sped away.

Soon they had turned off Chang'an Avenue and were heading to the Third Ring Road. Emily turned a dial on the radio. The police radio blared out in Mandarin.

"It's not about us," she said without turning to Hunter, who sat silently beside her.

"My name's Xiuying Tán. My father had been taken for re-education. I've been an MSS agent for the past two years. It was my job to bring you here and hand you over for interrogation. In return, my father would be released."

"So, all that stuff about Tsinghua University and being recruited by MI6 was a lie."

"I did attend Tsinghua University but was recruited by MSS, not MI6. I didn't have a choice. They have first-pick of the students who graduate. You don't turn them down."

"What did you do for them?"

"Code breaking. I'm a mathematics and computer science graduate."

"And the mind sieve worked, didn't it? You knew I wasn't Bruce Taylor."

"No. Everything I told you was true. I don't think the mind sieve is as effective as the government believe. You've got false memories it can't penetrate."

With a trace of dismay, Hunter said, "They put electrodes in my brain. I let them. Do you know who Bruce Taylor is?"

"No. I don't even know if he ever existed."

"And your father. You risked everything coming back for me."

Xiuying glanced across at him.

"I couldn't walk away and let them kill you," she said. "I thought I could but then, as I got to know you …"

"Do you love me?"

Xiuying shook her head.

"No. I said those things because I wanted to get my father back. But when I heard them beating you, I knew I couldn't leave you in there. It's not who I am. I can't trade your life for my father's, and I know he wouldn't want me to."

The car pulled up abruptly outside a brown-brick block of flats.

"Why have you stopped?" Hunter asked.

"There's a man in apartment 314. Tell him I sent you. He'll make you a new passport and get you on a flight back to England."

"So long, Xiuying Tán."

Xiuying leant forward and embraced Hunter.

"You take care of yourself, John Hunter."

Hunter got out, and Xiuying drove off.

Hunter wondered if he would ever see her again. She may not have loved him, but he loved her. Well, there was nothing to be done about that, he thought.

In one way, nothing had changed from when he had been Bruce Taylor. For Taylor, the past had not been personal—it had been something distant and abstract—and so it remained for him now. But one thing *had* changed. Unlike Taylor, he did not have an overpowering and crippling feeling of guilt. He felt no remorse for the countless people he had been assigned to eliminate. However, he had an obligation to try and make amends for the death of one person.

So, he would not be going back to England and MI5 but to Hamburg.

39

Charters stood, looking out of his office window, tapping his podgy fingers on the windowpane. The dark clouds parted to reveal a pale blue sky. It was going to be a beautiful day, he thought. He looked down at his chessboard, pleased. He had a winning position.

His desk phone rang, and he picked it up.

"Charters … I see … You're sure? Good. Don't let him out of your sight. What about Pritchard? I see. No, leave him for the moment."

He put the phone down and, allowing himself a smile, went back to the chessboard. A winning position, he thought. However, there were still a few more moves needed for checkmate.

Barnes emerged from Holborn station just as the sun was breaking through the cloud cover. There was still time, he thought. I mustn't give up hope.

He could not believe how Pritchard had just folded. When he had shown him the message that Anne had sent, there was a moment when Pritchard had been unable to breathe. It was as if the air had been sucked out of the room. He buried his face in his hands. After a moment, he had looked up at Barnes, his face flushed, tears standing in his eyes. Barnes had looked on as much in disgust as fear. All that talk of grit and determination about how Pritchard had worked his way up from the bottom had all been a lie. He was spineless. Well, *I'm* not going to give up, Barnes thought.

He had intercepted the message only ten minutes after Charters would have received it. They were probably still deciding what to do. It would be a straightforward matter with his false ID, Barnes thought, to get access to the safe deposit box, remove its contents, and then disappear.

He waited at the traffic lights. It was a busy day, the streets bustling with people. He glanced nervously around. No one looked familiar. He was sure he had not been followed.

If he had been better trained in surveillance work, he would have noticed the man wearing a black windbreaker, standing at a kiosk, who had been following him ever since he had arrived at Paddington.

Barnes walked briskly up the high street and went into the bank, confident of success. The man wearing the windbreaker took out his phone.

The front door of Pritchard's house was open, banging on its frame. Anderson tentatively pushed it open. A dim yellow light shone out into the hallway. He took a moment to listen but heard only the late evening creaks of the house. He went inside.

"Lewis?"

An eerie silence hung over everything. Anderson proceeded into the living room and caught his breath. Sitting directly across from the door was Pritchard, his face pallid in the lamplight. In his left hand was a half-finished tumbler of whiskey. His right hand was on his lap, clasping a small black gun. The ghost of a smile crossed his lips.

"I was wondering who they'd send," he said, his voice slurred, his eyes glassy.

He added, "I was hoping it would be you. I suppose they thought that our having worked together would give you a better chance?"

"Chance?" Anderson said.

"Of getting me to give myself up—to cooperate. Sit down."

Anderson glanced around the room. His body stiffened. In the far corner, Melissa was slumped in an armchair that had blood splattered over its upholstery.

"I didn't want to do it," Pritchard said. "But she gave me no choice. She was always uncooperative. Sit down."

Anderson sat down on the sofa across from Pritchard. He was in shock. He had come here because he had thought Pritchard was in danger. For a moment, the two men sat in silence, Pritchard taking the occasional sip from his glass.

"Where are my manners?" Pritchard said. "But then again, I never was much of a host. I always left that to Melissa. Would you like a drink?"

"No."

"Are you sure? I know how you and Sir Raymond are partial to a tipple."

Pritchard's thin lips twisted in a snarl of bitterness and defeat.

"Or is my booze not good enough for you Oxbridge types?"

"Is that what this is about?"

"You know what this is about. All that talk of queers at Black's bash. That was just to goad me, wasn't it? He knew. Both of you knew. You've been playing me from the start."

"It doesn't have to end here."

"I don't know why you'd want to stop me. This is better for you—for everyone. You get to avoid all the publicity. Do you really want me on TV, handcuffed and paraded before the world's media? Charters wouldn't like it—or his old chum, the PM.

"At least this way, people will remember me as an honest man, a man who fought against the odds and made something of his life. This way, my name won't be blackened.

"I made one mistake in my life. You don't know how it is. They say it's OK to be gay, but it isn't—especially when you don't have the old school tie. I would've been out the door in a heartbeat.

"I think I've had enough. You might want to look away. It's not going to be pretty."

Pritchard thrust the barrel of the gun into his mouth.

"No!" Anderson yelled.

Pritchard pulled the trigger.

40

Charters took a cigar from the wooden box on his desk and examined it.

"It's against regulations—even for me. But things couldn't have gone better. Are you sure you don't want one?"

"Yes, I'm sure," Anderson said.

Charters lit the cigar and puffed contentedly on it. He thumbed through a stack of eight-by-ten glossy photographs on his desk.

He said, "If only we'd got hold of these three years ago. We could've saved ourselves a lot of trouble."

"How long did you know about Melissa?"

"Poor Melissa. You mean about the whole marriage being fake. I was never a hundred per cent sure how she fitted in. I never could believe she had married him for love. You never had any suspicions?"

"No."

"He was like a cold fish. He did a good job of concealing who he really was. But these put the lie to that."

Charters patted the photographs on his desk.

Anderson said, "Brenner had them in a safe deposit box?"

"Yes. He'd been holding them as a kind of insurance for when he wanted out."

"May I have a look?"

"By all means."

Anderson picked up two photos from the stack. The black-and-white photographs of a bar, taken from CCTV cameras, were of good quality. The first was of Pritchard having a drink with a young man. The next one showed them kissing.

"These were taken during the Stonebridge op?" Anderson said,

"No, about six months before. The whole marriage was a sham to deflect attention away from his sexuality. Pritchard liked to portray himself as a man without passion or desires, but he secretly frequented gay bars in Old Compton Street."

"Why did Melissa agree to be his wife?"

"Blackmail—pure and simple. FSB was holding her son. They had Pritchard and were going to make sure he had whatever cover he needed to maintain his position. So, they set the whole thing up.

"To give Pritchard some credit, he was a reluctant mole. A lot of the intelligence he gave them was erroneous or simply out of date.

"He tipped off Brenner that we were going to move in to eliminate him. That was Taylor's death sentence. He never stood a chance when he arrived at Stonebridge. Pritchard always knew the man in the hospital was an imposter because he knew the Russians had killed Taylor.

"The man in the hospital was John Hunter. He was the first one we recruited for Clean Start. Taylor was recruited a few months later. Like Taylor, he was a ruthless assassin. But things went wrong; the electrodes hadn't been fitted correctly. Even the slightest misalignment can cause problems. After an incident where he was hit by a car, instead of feeling no remorse or empathy, he suffered from extreme guilt and found it difficult to come to terms with what he was and all the people he had killed.

"He suffered a complete mental breakdown. We had him treated in the best hospitals, but he was a lost cause, and we had to have him institutionalized. He didn't have any close family, and he wasn't one to make friends, so no one kicked up a fuss. We kept him on ice. You never know when you'll need your assets again."

"And then Brenner left his message at Stonebridge?"

"Yes. It was a long shot that he would ever call, but I kept the line open just in case. It wasn't easy to keep everything from Pritchard. I had to set up a whole team in-house. I knew Pritchard wasn't working alone—he had to be part of a network.

"I'm sorry that I kept you in the dark about everything. I couldn't take even the slither of a chance. I did a lot of the work myself, setting up Hunter's reappearance at the hospital. I haven't worked this hard since I was out in the field. Of course, Henley did all the work manipulating Hunter's memories and implanting the keywords: Stonebridge and Clean Start.

"I would have liked to have got Hunter and Brenner back alive. Their deaths are the only black mark on this whole op."

"Them and Anne."

"Oh, yes, Anne."

"You haven't heard anything?"

"No. We'll have to talk to the Russians about repatriating her body."

"So, the whole Chinese angle was just a diversion—like your game of chess."

Charters smiled.

"My priority was to expose Pritchard's network, but I thought I could kill two birds with one stone and learn more about their mind sieve technology. There was never any risk of exposure regarding Clean Start. Henley did a thorough job on Hunter. If the mind sieve does work, they'll extract false memories telling them that Clean Start was a programme that targeted Chinese sleeper cells, and that's all."

"So, if we get intelligence telling us that's what they believe, it'll be confirmation that the mind sieve works."

"Exactly."

"And Belkovsky?"

"As soon as Pritchard heard about Taylor's reappearance, he must have called his Russian handlers, and they sent him in— the imposter Belkovsky, that is."

"And Black's bash. All that talk about queers. You were baiting him?"

"Yes, I probably did go too far, but I wanted to see how he'd react. I was hoping that he would make contact with the other moles. I had suspected a few people in K Division but not Barnes. He was a bonus.

"The only time I got a bit unnerved was when you started your own investigations. I personally swapped Hunter's photograph with Taylor's, but I forgot about the watermark. It's a good thing Pritchard didn't look at the file. He would have noticed it too."

"These photos in the bar were all the leverage the Russians had on him?"

"Yes. Of course, his sexuality was never an issue."

"But he didn't see it that way."

"No, you know how he was. It was always him against the world. If he had come straight to us and told us that he might have been compromised, we would have helped him."

"What's going to happen to Barnes?"

"No decision's been made. The Americans are interested, and there's been talk of rendition. Publicity's not a problem because of his low profile."

"And Pritchard's suicide is the same?"

"Yes. He didn't have much of a public profile. He kept away from the press. It's a pity he had to kill Melissa."

"I don't think he ever told her anything. I'm sure she hated him. Margaret said as much to me. It was his one last act of defiance."

Anderson handed the photographs back and slumped down in his chair.

"Is anything the matter?" Charters asked. "You don't seem yourself."

Anderson felt foolish and clumsier than ever. Charters had kept him out of the loop, and yet, he had still nearly ruined the whole op.

"I've got a meeting with the DG tomorrow," he said. "I'm going to hand in my resignation."

Charters leant back in his chair.

"This is all out of the blue. Why?"

"I just feel it's time to hand over the baton. Give the new generation, the Wheelers of this world, a chance to show what they can do."

"This isn't anything to do with what I said at the party, is it?"

Anderson frowned in perplexity.

"That stuff about us being old duffers?" Charters said.

"No," Anderson said.

"Then what? This op's been a big success. We got our man, and we've turned up a lot more under that dirty rock."

"We can't go on forever, Raymond. I just want to get out while I'm still ahead."

"Well, I didn't see this coming, but I respect your decision. As long as you're making it for the right reasons."

"I am," Anderson said. "I am."

41

Doctor Iliyas Omarov put the X-ray negative onto the lightbox, pressed the switch, and let out a sigh as the light flickered. He banged the side of the box, and the light flickered several more times until it settled and became a constant glow.

He thought of the modern hospitals he had seen on American TV shows, their equipment new and reliable. Out here on the border of Kazakhstan, they were still using equipment dating back to the Soviet era. Indeed, the lightbox had a faded CCCP stamp on its frame.

Iliyas rubbed his eyes and turned as he heard the soft footsteps of an approaching nurse.

"The patient has regained consciousness," she said.

"Has she said anything?"

"Yes, but I didn't understand. I think she's English."

Iliyas turned back to study the X-ray negative.

"Interesting," he said.

"Will we have to amputate the leg?" the nurse asked indifferently.

Iliyas glanced back at her.

"I'll talk it over with Dr Azamat. I'll need to see if there's any infection. But the X-ray is encouraging. There are only clean breaks, nothing crushed. She was very lucky."

Five minutes later, Iliyas entered the ward. Anne was asleep. She was one of six patients in a ward that smelt of damp and mildew. The rusty metal-framed beds squeaked as the patients groaned and shifted, restlessly turning. We don't even have enough drugs to make life tolerable for them, Iliyas lamented. At least the new patient was resting.

He was a little disappointed that she was not awake. He would have liked to talk to her, but he knew that with all the drugs and painkillers she had been given, it would have been unlikely she would have been lucid. Even so, he wanted to practise his English. He had been learning it now for over a year but had no opportunity out here to practise it with a native speaker. If she was American, he would ask her about the hospitals in California. He would very much like to work there one day. He would take his wife to see the golden beaches and the blue waters of San Francisco Bay.

Anne lay flat on her back, her leg encased in a metal frame, large screws bolted through the bones. A rugged-faced man came into the ward, drying his hands on his dirty jeans.

"How is she, doctor?"

"You're the man who found her?"

"Yes. It was pure luck. I was late coming back from a hunting trip. If it hadn't been so dark, I would have driven straight past and not seen the headlights. Another thirty minutes and the battery would have been flat, and there wouldn't even have been that."

"I think she'll pull through. She's been very lucky. You saved her life."

The man smiled and stroked his beard.

Iliyas added, "I'll let her know what happened when she regains consciousness. I'll tell her what you did."

"Not necessary. It's enough that she's alive. My wife wanted to be sure that she would live. She thinks it would be bad luck if she died. She's from Taraz. You know what a superstitious lot they are."

The man left. Iliyas remained by Anne's bed. There was nothing to do but wait. He glanced out of the window. The snow was falling heavily. Temperatures could drop to forty below. She must be a real fighter, he thought, to have survived such conditions. Her good fortune was not only that she was alive but that the hunter had not caused any permanent damage to her leg when he had removed her from the car.

Anne dreamt of her rescue. She was succumbing to the cold and had lost feeling in most of her body. Then, a light had been shone in her face. Slowly, she opened her eyes. The concerned face of the hunter, his beard frosted white, emerged from the blizzard of snow. There followed a moment of delirium when he lifted her from the car, and she had thought he was an angel taking her to heaven.

She awoke from her dream. Iliyas was standing with his back to her, reading her medical notes. She was warm and safe. She had really made it out of the car.

She had not dreamt about her husband since she had been brought into the hospital. She would dream of him again; she would never forget him. However, she felt her dreams would no longer leave her feeling empty and alone. She had a new, full life ahead of her. Life had never felt so precious. She closed her eyes and dreamt of being back in her warm flat. The next time Tom Sutherland asked her out to dinner, she would keep her date with him.

Printed in Great Britain
by Amazon